I0545353

Vampire Prince

Magical Academy

Lina Bengston

Published by Lina Bengston, 2021.

VAMPIRE PRINCE

First edition. October 6, 2021.

ISBN: 978-1735549255

Written by Lina Bengston.

Book Description

Vampire Prince
I thought the knowledge of my past would solve my problems... boy, was I wrong.

IF ONLY I COULD RETURN to a time when my life was simple. Things were less complicated in those days. Now, my life is in danger, and I'm not sure what supernatural race is after me.

Luckily, I have the support of my Shifter heir boyfriends. But, against more powerful enemies, we need the Vampire heir and the Caster heir on our side. However, this complicates our relationship a great deal.

The heirs must come together soon, or we will not survive the constant attacks we face.

·VIOLENCE, FOUL LANGUAGE, and Adult contents included.

Content warning

This book contains disturbing materials that readers might find not to their liking.

Chapter 1

Vi

WEEKS HAD PASSED, BUT still no word from my mates. I spent my day pacing Kol's apartment, moving from room to room like a caged animal itching to get out but fearful of being discovered.

The phone Sebastian gave me made a permanent imprint on my hand as it hasn't left my possession, hoping someone would call, or at least send me a quick message, but nothing.

Even gazing outside the window to admire the view from above didn't hold my attention like it usually would.

As I sat on Kol's bed, I reached for my necklace that held my parents' wedding rings and my mom's ashes and closed my eyes in an effort to calm down, but my mind churned with worry. With a deep breath, I tried reaching out to Sebastian and Tristan through our mate bond even though I was warned against it.

I was done waiting. I needed to know they were okay. Plus, I was beginning to question if I had just dreamt out mating as a coping mechanism to my mother's loss. Thank goodness our bond snapped into place whenever I shifted into my wolf form and I could feel them as strongly as if they were in the next room. So lately, I had been shifting often to keep my sanity.

With a sigh, I glanced at the clock and gave up on my attempt in reaching them. It was almost dinner time, and I planned to question the person who delivered the food about Kol's whereabouts. I hadn't seen him in over twenty-four hours and it concerned me because he had been acting cagey lately. However, whoever brought me food often disappeared whenever I opened the door.

With a couple of minutes left, I waited quietly.

Maybe I should stand by the door?

My legs bounced in anticipation, but I caught myself since a Vampire would pick up on the noise, but I couldn't do anything about my racing heartbeat.

The clock slowly ticked to six, and sure enough, I heard a knock. I jumped up and quickly opened the door. However, all I saw was a blur.

Dammit. Why was the person avoiding me?

I eyed the food cart and the empty hall and followed even though Kol had given me strict instructions to stay put. However, if I didn't get out of that room, I would scream.

My footsteps echoed across the winding hall, even though I tried to make my steps on the cement as light as possible.

I'd been walking for a few minutes, but there was no end to these endless corners. Careful not to be seen, I stuck close to the torch-lit wall. Finally, after rounding another curve, I bounded down several flights of stairs, stopping to brace my weight and catch my breath on the cold cobblestone wall at the bottom of the stairs as I glanced both ways to more empty halls.

The fluorescent light buzzed as I walked past and the air smelled stale, which gave me the impression that I was underground.

They lined the hall with rooms of different sizes with opaque windows as I ducked under as I passed each room.

I didn't dare open the doors until my steps halted at faint voices ahead which had me leaning against the wall and glancing on both sides of the hall, still clear of Vampires.

I inched closer to the voices and saw a door open.

I didn't want to alert them, but I was sure their Vampire senses would pick up on me if I moved. Should I backtrack or speak with someone? What if they were avoiding me, or worse, what if they attacked? I was certain I could defend myself, so I took a chance and tapped into my Vampire speed and blurred to the door.

A redhead drew a gun before any of the other guys even realized what was going on. Damn, this chick was fast.

Before I ducked my head and raised my hand, her eyes grew in recognition, and she holstered her gun. "How can I help you, Violet?"

I dropped my hands, which were getting ready to gesture to her not to shoot. "You know who I am?" I let out a breath of relief.

"Of course. I'm Amelia, and these are my men." She gestured to four large men behind her.

"Hello, Amelia. Do you know where I can find Kol?"

There was a brief hesitation in her expression before wiping it clear. "He's with his father, and he should be back this evening. How about I walk you back to the apartment?"

I eyed her for a moment but couldn't read her expression, so I sighed in defeat. "Sure, I guess."

We walked in silence as she walked at a brisk pace that I struggled to keep up with.

"I think it's safer. You never know who might lurk in the hall." She glanced over her shoulder.

"Do you have an update on what's going on outside?" I asked, catching up with her as she slowed to a stop in front of Kol's door.

"Uh, it's best for you to discuss it with Kol." Her eyes shifted as she scratched her brow. Then she smiled and said, "Don't leave, okay? I'll send Kol up as soon as I see him."

I stepped inside, not bothering to answer.

Stupid. I should have gone down the other hallway. Since the halls were mostly empty, I would try again tomorrow. I needed to get out and get news about my mates.

I ate my dinner slowly as I trained my eyes on the front door. I didn't move, even after my plate had long been empty, hoping that Kol would walk in any minute, but he didn't. I shoved off my seat with a heavy sigh and went straight to Kol's bed, not bothering to change, determined to wait for him. I stared at the ceiling for what felt like hours, but I must have dozed off since I woke up with a start and found Kol leaning on the door with his arms crossed.

"Hey."

His pupils grew, and his mouth lifted in a smile, but then he quickly stiffened. "Hey. I heard you were looking for me."

I sat on the edge of the bed and looked up at him. "Yes. I'm going crazy here, Kol." I pushed up and advanced closer, but I noticed his hard expression, so I stopped.

What was his problem?

"I need to know how they're doing. Please tell me if they're okay. I can't just stay locked up indefinitely, not knowing how they are."

His eyes softened, and he moved to take a step closer but changed his mind. "It's why I was gone so long. Tristan and Sebastian are still in hiding with King Rahl while the Casters remain relentless with their attack and their demand that they turn you in."

"Oh, God. This needs to stop." I sat back heavily on the bed. My brow crumpled as I looked around helplessly, as if a miracle would present itself to me in Kol's room. "I should just go to them." I looked up at him but didn't meet his eyes.

He sat next to me and said, "Listen to me, Vi. You can't give in. The Casters can't have you. If they do, they will use you as their weapon, and they'll be unstoppable. Do you understand?"

I didn't answer. I knew he was right, but I was tired of being locked up with no one to talk to.

How did this become my life? I ran my hand over my hair in frustration, but then guilt filled me as I thought of the Shifters risking their lives to protect me. I blinked away tears and turned away from Kol. I didn't want him to see my conflicting feelings, since I knew I was being selfish.

"Hey, I know it's hard. Just hang in there longer." He pulled me close, and it was like a dam opened. Tears poured out of me, and my shoulders shook. Kol held me stiffly and rubbed my back as he murmured reassurances.

I buried my face closer, needing his comfort.

"I'm sorry you're going through this, and I've been little help. I promise to keep you posted and be here more. Okay?"

I nodded, not letting go.

Kol must have sensed that I needed him since he pulled me to bed and held me until I fell asleep. It was the first time I had a good night's sleep in days.

Kol

"AMELIA, ANY NEWS?"

"Yes. Nothing good." Her troubled eyes met mine. "The Casters attacked another Shifter safe house yesterday, resulting in casualties on both sides. Although there is discord within the Casters, the main coven remains strong because they draw strength from the entire race. Not to mention Vampires are getting anxious. We've been breaking up fights most nights about this war."

I nodded, but none of what she said was new to me.

"What about the King?" she asked.

"Father still doesn't want to get involved, and the Queen keeps pushing to side with the Casters."

She halted in front of me. "That can't happen, Kol."

"I know that!" I snapped. "Why do you think I've been spending so much time with him?" I sighed and said in a calmer voice, "I haven't had to spend this much time with my father since I was a child, so I could convince him to side with the Shifters."

"So what's the hold-up? It's not like he cares."

I shook my head. "That's the thing. He doesn't care, and he keeps going on and on about other nonsensical shit. Every time I bring it up, the bitch keeps blocking my attempts."

"It's imperative you try, Kol. The Queen can't get her way."

"I know. I'm trying to formulate a plan."

There was silence as we stewed on our situation. "Any additional information on your mission?"

She shook her head dismissively. "No. It's complicated. However, I have a lead I'm following up on. It might take a while, but if it pans out, it will turn the tides on this war."

I examined her for a moment. I trust her with my life, and I knew she was the best, so I didn't push. "Keep me posted, will you?"

"You'll be the first to know."

I got up to leave, but then Amelia called after me, "Oh, Kol? You need to take care of your little problem. If you don't keep a closer eye on her, next time, she will find her way outside, and I might not be there to stop her." She held my eyes until I nodded.

She was right, and I needed to keep a close eye on Vi. Plus, I promised her I would be around more often. Although, it was getting more difficult each day. I needed to find a solution to my problem before it was too late.

Chapter 2

Kol

AS I WALKED THROUGH the tunnels, the rhythmic tune of my footfalls provided solace from my insatiable hunger for Vi's blood. It had been a couple of weeks since I last fed, but no matter what I tried, I couldn't feed.

It was my stupid fault—a rookie mistake.

Although it was the first time I had drunk straight from the vein, I couldn't blame my lack of control on my inexperience. There was something about Vi's blood that had provoked me to lose my carefully constructed self-restraint. Since I first laid eyes on her, I felt drawn to her; something I had never felt towards anyone.

It was as if my subconscious wanted to claim her, and now I had forced the bond.

My fists clenched, my nails digging into my skin at the thought.

She didn't even like Vampires, although she didn't seem to mind me, and sometimes I think she might even like me.

I ran a shaky hand over my face.

My mouth tasted like cotton, and my throat felt scratchy and raw as I tried to think of anything I hadn't tried, aside from drinking blood from different batches, drinking it warm or cold, or mixing it with food. I even plugged my nose and made myself swallow the bottled blood, but I just threw it all up.

I was fucking starving and short-tempered as I faced my vile stepmother. If she sniffed even a hint of weakness at me, she would take advantage, so I needed to make sure not to give her any ammo against me.

I considered having my guards go with me, but that would raise suspicion, so I went alone.

I paused and took a few calming breaths and cleared my expression before I stepped through the iron door of the castle. In a matter of minutes, I was striding out the hidden door that would take me to the King and Queen's private chambers.

With my chin held high, I gazed at my father, who didn't look me in the eye, then at my evil stepmother, who, unsurprisingly, eyed me with disdain.

"You called?" I asked in a monotone voice as I kept my balled hands in my trousers. I met her cold, calculating eyes with a bland look, something I had perfected when I was young.

We played this power game for years. It began when I realized I was stronger than her. After all, I was an heir, and she wasn't supposed to be queen. She took advantage of an opportunity and snaked her way into my mother's spot. Therefore, she didn't gain the power that came with the position. The only power she had was the vileness seeping from her pores.

I didn't think my father had feelings for her. I was certain he was past caring, or her foulness blinded him since he had given up on life when he lost my mother. I've seen moments of the man he could have been, and it was always when the evil wench wasn't by his side. This wouldn't be the day I got to speak with my father. He was but a shell.

"Thanks for coming, Kol. The war is getting worse, and our people are caught in the middle, demanding we make a stand," he said in a bored voice as he glanced at the Queen briefly. It didn't take a genius to know that she was the one pressing to take sides. It also wasn't news that she hated Shifters.

I kept my expression neutral and waited since I didn't want to show the Queen who I supported in this war.

"I would like your opinion on the matter before I decide." The King leaned back, resting his arms on the wooden arm of his chair by the fireplace.

"Why do we need to take sides? This isn't our fight. If we do, humans will take notice. Shouldn't that be our priority?" I asked, keeping my voice impartial.

The Queen chortled before I even finished speaking. The hairs on my arms stood, and I had to take a quick breath in as I reminded myself to unclench my jaw—long gone was the child who yearned for this woman's affection.

I saw past her facade. She pretended to be a loving mother in front of my father, grandfather, and the court. But behind closed doors, I endured years of abuse—something I wouldn't forget.

I wasted my formative years as I strived to be perfect but always fell short, crying myself to sleep, asking what I did wrong and why she didn't love me. Each day, fresh determination filled me as I pushed myself to do better, wishing that if I did something different, she wouldn't loathe me, or I wouldn't suffer her wrath, until I grew up and realized she was vile and weak.

The only love I felt was from Florence, my nursemaid who passed away five years ago. If it weren't for her, I would have turned out to be a monster, but she told me stories about my kind-hearted mother despite the Queen's order and raised me as if I were her own. She nursed me to health each time the Queen got her hands on me and taught me how to be strong, pick myself up, and fight during the bleakest times. She also taught me how to control my emotions and not give the Queen any leverage against me.

It was because of Florence I found the courage to stand up to Queen Delia.

I would never forget the fear in the Queen's eyes the day I fought back and released my powers. Since then, she stopped coming at me directly. She must have realized she would never beat me directly, so her attacks had become more calculated—I take pleasure in knowing that she wasn't confident my father would take her side. However, she was cunning enough in my father's absent state, so I never discounted the power she held over the kingdom. I knew she was still a dangerous opponent. That was why I still watched my steps around her as I bid my time until I took the bitch out.

"Of course we need to take sides, dear boy. Otherwise, our adversaries would think us weak. Isn't that right, Henry?" She reached over and touched my father's arm.

He glanced at their touching skin in confusion.

She pulled her hand away like it had burned her when she didn't get the reaction she had intended. I wanted to smirk, but

I kept my expression neutral. She flashed me a glare, but I met her eyes straight on until she broke eye contact.

What power coursed through my father's veins, I felt in mine. As the only Vampire heir, I felt my father's power transfer to me slowly throughout the years. I didn't think he was weakening, but I did think he was giving up hope. The death of my mother, his mate, had killed something inside of him, and the power needed an outlet.

"Father, I have issued a firm command to my men not to take sides, or they will answer to me. Of course, I will rescind that command based on your decision, my King," I said with a slight bow of my head. I didn't miss the death glare the Queen flashed me.

"No, I agree, son. Where is my scribe?" He gestured.

"Sire." Mr. Tibult bowed.

"Issue this statement to our people. Anyone who is caught taking sides in this war will be arrested. By order of the King. No one will supersede my command." He gestured impatiently for Mr. Tibult to leave.

My eyes darted to the Queen, whose face was red with rage.

"Father, if you require nothing else. I will take my leave." I bowed.

"Thank you, Kol." He pushed off the seat and left the room without a backward glance to anyone. I strolled out the side exit, waiting for the Queen to call me back. I was ready for her to scream at me or threaten me, but it never came, which made me warier. She was more dangerous when she was plotting than when she was visibly angry. *Fuck!* Now, I had to be extra careful.

I took one of the secret passages that led to my tower and went straight to the command center on the outskirts of the castle built by my father and Uncle Dante—another heir and my father's cousin who was closer than a brother to him.

The day I fought against my stepmother was the first time I realized I had my father's powers. Something might have awoken in my blood since it was also the same day Amanda and Deacon approached me.

Amanda was a tech genius and the head of surveillance, while Deacon was the head of intel. They held the same position when my father and Uncle Dante built the tower. They took an oath to my father and agreed to be bound to the tower, protect the current heir, and train the heir's elite guards.

That night, they had moved me to the tower, along with Florence. They had assured me that, after my mother's death, they had made sure that the wards on every inch of this structure and the tunnels were foolproof. Even Casters wouldn't be able to break the enchantments since they imbued it with both Vampire blood and magic.

"Kol. What can we do for you?" Amanda turned from her computer while Deacon nodded his head and continued to type away.

"Almost done. One more second," Deacon murmured as Amanda gazed at him with adoration.

Deacon finally turned from the screen and smiled at me with tired eyes. "What's up?"

"Anything I should worry about?" I asked.

He shook his head. "No. I'm just making sure no one knows about our little visitor upstairs. I'm constantly making sure I keep up with the current chatter."

"What can we do for you, Kol?" Amanda poured three glasses of blood whiskey and handed me a drink.

"Hey, Kol," Amelia said as she sat next to Deacon. She was the perfect blend of her parents—a tech genius and had a knack for getting intel on anyone: a super spy. Amelia had surpassed her parents in skills. She was a badass and kicked any of my elite guards' asses. She was my best friend, and we grew up together. If she didn't hate school, she would have been at the academy, protecting me. Instead, she stayed and did what she did best: spy on the Queen on my behalf.

I nodded and grabbed the glass hesitantly and swirled the contents as I stared at it with apprehension. I took a tentative sip to see if I would gag, but I felt fine, so I took a bigger drink. Then I felt my stomach turn. I stood abruptly and ran to the sink as I spat out the whiskey.

"What have you done, Kol?" Amelia leaned over the sink.

I glanced at her sideways as I hovered over the sink, still dry heaving. Her arms crossed over her usual leather attire.

I rinsed off my mouth and didn't respond. Instead, I made my way back to the round table where Amanda and Deacon sat waiting patiently. I plopped on the seat, feeling my limbs shake.

"Kol, tell me whose ass I should kick." Amelia's eyes flashed in anger.

"Language," Deacon admonished.

"Kol. Tell us what's going on." Amanda moved closer and felt my forehead. Not that Vampires got sick, but it was her motherly instincts kicking in. After Florence passed, she took it upon herself to always ask how I was doing. She had raised me alongside Amelia.

I rubbed my eyes with the heels of my hands and sighed. "I haven't eaten in a couple of weeks. I've tried everything. I can't keep anything down." I buried my head in my arms on the table and allowed myself a moment of weakness. These guys were my family, and I could be weak for a moment. I was tired and hungry, and I just needed a second.

Amanda rubbed my back. The comfort provided almost brought tears to my eyes. I got little affection, especially a motherly touch, and today, I needed it. Amelia must have sensed how much I was hurting because she was uncharacteristically quiet.

"Kol, please tell me you didn't?" she whispered.

I chuckled, then lifted my head and met her eyes. I knew she couldn't help it. She couldn't keep her mouth shut. Plus, with a genius-level IQ like hers, I knew she would figure it out.

"What? What am I missing?" Deacon asked.

"Ask the idiot." Amelia waved her hand in my direction.

"I didn't do it on purpose!" I snapped. Amelia and I always argued. She brought out the competitive side of me. "We needed to escape the Casters, and she had a panic attack. It was an accident." I shrugged.

"Oh, please, Kol. It was not an accident." Amelia crossed her arms and flashed me a look that I knew so well. She was daring me to contradict her.

I narrowed my eyes, then shook my head. "Fine. I fucking tasted her blood. I wanted to bond with her, and I don't regret it." As the words left my mouth, I knew it was true. I wanted the bond. Even though I didn't plan on it, the bond formed on its own because it knew what I wanted. Fuck.

"Could it be?" Amanda asked.

"Perhaps." Deacon shrugged.

My gaze snapped between the couples. I looked at Amelia in question, but she only stared at me with disapproval.

"I don't care if you've met your mate. You can't be weakened at a time like this. The Queen is planning something. I don't know the details, but it makes me nervous, so you need to be in your best shape." She marched forward.

"Wait. What? What are... What do you mean, *mate*?"

She stopped in front of me with her hands on her hips. "Don't tell me it didn't cross your mind."

"Well. Yeah, but she's a Shifter." I shrugged.

"Yeah, but our intel says she has mimic and siphon powers. Shifters don't have that kind of power." Deacon raised his brow.

My eyes widened. I was both impressed and worried that he knew Vi's secret.

"This is not the immediate problem!" Amelia snapped.

"What do you recommend?" I shot back.

"Tilt your head back."

"I don't want to throw up again. I just threw up my guts not too long ago. I'm worried I'll be throwing up my stomach next."

"Just trust me, okay?" she said with extreme patience.

I eyed her skeptically, which she only returned with an eye roll while her hand rested on her hip. "Okay, I'll drip some fresh blood, and Dad will plug your nose until you swallow, and you will chase it down with some plain water. We'll do this a little at a time. This will be a sacrifice on my part because I'll need to cut my freaking wrist open constantly, so if this works, you owe me big!"

"Can you collect after we see if it works?"

"Fine. Lean back."

I scooted further down my seat and leaned my head back.

"Open up."

I felt blood drip onto my tongue, and already my gut reaction was to recoil from it, which was unusual for a Vampire. So I just kept my mouth open and cleared my mind. I allowed it to flow to the back of my throat, and as soon as it pooled, I felt Deacon plug my nose. I didn't have a choice but to swallow. Amanda handed me a glass of water, which I gulped down. I felt queasy, but I didn't run to the sink. I could feel my body already reacting to the blood. Even if it was only a tiny amount, it was like getting a shot of adrenalin. I felt great!

"Should we do one more? How are you feeling? I don't want to do too much at the risk of you throwing it up." Amelia eyed me closely.

"I feel queasy, so maybe we should stop. Let's see if I keep this down. If it works, then we can increase it next time. This is a good start. I feel better already. Thanks, Amelia." I got up and hugged her.

"Don't worry. I will collect once this is all over. Now, go figure this shit out before I need to move into your tower and keep a closer eye on you."

"Oh, God, no. Let me get on with that. Anything just to make sure that doesn't happen." I raised my hand and rubbed her head with my knuckles.

She ducked and tried to punch my arm. I avoided her punch, and I hugged Amanda and tapped Deacon's shoulder before waving goodbye.

They were right. I needed to work on my connection with Vi. I couldn't be weak, or I wouldn't be able to protect her.

Chapter 3

Vi

SOMETHING WAS WRONG with Kol. I previously suspected he was avoiding me, but now I was sure of it. When we exchanged words, he wouldn't look me in the eye and would only grunt out minimum responses then leave the room in a hurry.

He promised he would be around more, but he had been scarcer. I spent more time glancing at the damn phone, terrified of receiving horrible news. I imagined awful scenarios of my mates getting injured.

I couldn't lose any of them, not even Rahl or Carlisle. I couldn't lose any more people in my life; I just couldn't. I clutched at my necklace and glanced out the window.

I hadn't changed out of my clothes in two days. My mind had been racing, and the sleep I had gotten was just a few hours at most when my body would shut down involuntarily. Kol was called to the castle a couple of days ago, and he hadn't been in the same room as me since then.

At least Amelia checked on me before going to check on Kol.

I hadn't left his room, hoping he would come back, needing something, but he didn't.

Today, I was determined for Kol to speak with me, so I jumped in the shower and changed into leggings and a T-shirt—courtesy of Amelia. She had bought me the essentials, so at least I didn't have to wear Kol's clothes. I didn't bother drying my hair. I marched towards the room Kol had been staying in.

Did I knock and give him a chance to turn me away or just barge in? What if he was naked? I moved to grab the handle and paused, my fingers curled into a fist. I took a deep breath and straightened my back, then barged into the room.

The door opened with a bang, and I paused just a few steps in. It took my eyesight a while to adjust to the darkness. For a moment, I hesitated, unsure if Kol was inside.

Then I saw a shaky, pale hand wave me away, and Kol's voice croaked, "Vi. Please leave."

I rushed to his side. "Oh my God. What's wrong? Are you sick? Why didn't you say?" I climbed on the bed and touched his gaunt face, but he turned away.

What the hell? He looked like he was on his deathbed. I blindly reached for the light and gasped at Kol's sunken red eyes. I take it back. He looked like a corpse.

"What the fuck?" I lifted his shirt to check for injury, but his skin was intact, and I didn't see any parts of him bleeding. "Tell me what's going on, now."

"Please leave. I can't..."

"No. I am not letting you die."

"I can't control it."

"What are you talking about?"

His fangs descended, and my heart sped. My mind raced to the alley when my mother died, but I quickly realized that Kol must be hungry. I trusted him with my life, so I offered my wrist to him.

But he scrunched up his eyes in shame.

"Kol. You fucking listen to me right now. You must eat. I won't let you die because of pride. Eat."

"You don't understand."

I leaned over to hear him better since his fangs strangled his words as he clamped his lips shut.

"I don't care. You're not dying."

In response, he turned his back on me and curled up in a fetal position. His sweaty shirt clung to his frame, which outlined bones and skin instead of his usually muscly body.

I knew I could overpower the stubborn ass and make him drink my blood. So what was the best way to do that? If I gave him my wrist, I wouldn't be able to hold him down with my hands.

I tied my hair up in a bun. Then, in one move, I had Kol straddled, with both his hands above his head. I leaned forward, offering my neck to him.

I felt him buck and shake his head, and I heard muffled words. It sounded like his fangs had descended once again. I felt my left hand partially shift, and with my sharp claws, I carefully slashed at my neck and pressed closer to Kol.

He froze under me, and I knew I had him. In just moments, his fangs pierced my skin, and then I felt him suck and pull my blood into his mouth.

A loud moan escaped me as heat pooled in my belly. I ground my hips and found Kol's hard length pressing into me.

Yes. Right where I needed him. I continued rotating my hips, chasing the ache that had slowly built.

The demand inside of me increased. I needed him to finish what he started.

As if he had read my mind, he flipped us, and losing his mouth on mine had me crying out. However, he quickly moved his mouth back to my lips, demanding, as if he needed my oxygen to breathe.

I tasted the tang of blood as my tongue met his lips, which I found enticing. My hips jerked forward, which he met, drawing another moan from my mouth.

My hands greedily roamed his back, scratching and tugging him close to me. A deep, animalistic urgency inside of me had awoken, and I needed Kol or I felt like I would die. He must have suffered the same intense craving because he ripped my shirt and bra off and devoured my breasts with his mouth and hands. Then he did the same to my leggings and panties as his mouth latched on to my clit, which had me bursting. Without waiting to recover, he was inside of me.

Just within moments, I felt like I was going to come again. Then he bit into the other side of my neck, and I could have sworn I passed out at how powerful my orgasm was. He continued to drink my blood, but the magnitude of our passion had waned. Now I could think around my need for him.

So had Kol. He slowed down and sat me on top of him as we gazed into each other's eyes and rocked slowly. My heart sailed at the way he stared into my soul. It was like we were one. Our union was no longer about the physical act, but our souls danced in a complicated rhythm, rejoicing over being united. I could feel his essence in every fiber of my being, just like I had with the princes. We belonged together—all of us.

I felt myself slowly build, and when I felt my climax, my Vampire fangs descended and I bit into his shoulder. I heard him grunt as he came with me.

"Fuck! Vi. I..."

I seized his face and kissed him slowly as I felt our bond lock into place. I'd always known we were connected. I just didn't think we could be mates since he was a Vampire and I was a Shifter. Shit. What would Tristan and Sebastian say?

Kol brushed the hair off my face and stared deep into my eyes. "What's wrong? Do you regret..."

I kissed him before he could finish his sentence. "Never think that. I was just worried about what Tristan and Seb would say. In a different situation, I would have preferred to talk to them before..." I shrugged.

He grazed his lips on my forehead. "I understand." Then he captured my mouth. I sensed him twitch under me. I released his lips and glanced between us, and sure enough, he was ready to go again. I raised a brow and grinned.

His beautiful green eyes shone with amusement. His face was no longer sunken. His body was back to its regular firmness. "Can you blame me? I've been dying to do that since the moment I laid eyes on you, and I've been starving since I first tasted your blood." He moved to kiss me once again, but I leaned back.

"What do you mean you've been starving?"

"When I bit you the first time, I accidentally injected my venom into you, and I couldn't stand drinking others' blood. Heirs are forbidden because it forms a certain bond between

Vampires, and it's risky for heirs because if it's unrequited, it might mean death for us and end our line." He shrugged nonchalantly.

"Why didn't you tell me?" The ass. He was willing to die rather than just ask for blood?

"I didn't want to pressure you into anything."

What kind of foolish reasoning was that? I frowned. "Don't ever jeopardize your life like that again."

"Yes, ma'am. I'm sorry. Let me make it up to you." He captured my lips and kissed me gently, which drove me mad.

He continued the slow lick and nipped down my neck, then continued down my chest, spending some time on each breast. By the time he passed my stomach, and I felt his breath on my clit, my hips jerked in impatience as I firmly gripped the sheets. It didn't take long before I cried his name. My legs shook, and I needed a minute to recover, but Kol was commanding in bed, which I loved. He was also ravenous, and his bite was becoming one of my favorites.

"Bite me." I exhaled. He obliged by biting the top of my breast, which had me clenching down. Kol wasn't kidding. I lost count on how many positions he had tried and how many orgasms he rang out of me.

At one point, he inserted a finger inside my ass, which made me freeze in surprise. "I intend on fucking every inch of you," he whispered, which replaced any hesitation I had into a quivering desire. Kol brought out a lustful vixen in me. I liked whatever he did to my body. Even ass play. I didn't think I would be into it, but I ended up loving it.

It was way past lunch when he finally let me rest. He carried me to his room and drew a bath, taking longer than necessary since he couldn't get enough of our coupling. However, as soon as he moved me to his bed, I was asleep as soon as I hit the pillow. My last thought was how sweet he was as he wrapped me in his arms and pulled me close.

I awoke to feelings of warmth and safety and, for a change, I was well-rested. I gasped as my whole body felt tingly. It was sensitive to the touch, but in a good way. Then I felt fingers between my thighs, and my eyes opened.

"Morning." Kol kissed behind my ears as his hand cupped my breast, then roamed to my stomach and back down between my legs. "Are you always dripping wet when you wake up?" he whispered as he pushed a finger inside me.

I gasped but I couldn't move as he had my back pinned against his body, pushing against his hardness.

"I love how my mate can keep up with me. I'm voracious when it comes to your blood and your body," he murmured as his finger circled my clit, causing shivers down my spine. "Tell me how you want to come. Bite." He nipped at my shoulder, which I arched in anticipation. "Finger." He rubbed slowly, which made my hips thrust. "Or cock?" He entered and pumped a few times, which hit a spot that had me pushing against him and crying out when he pulled out. "Tell me, my little vixen."

I was gasping as his ministrations filled my foggy brain with lust. I was so close I couldn't think. "I just want to come." I exhaled.

"Perhaps you wanted to come another way." He inserted a finger in my ass, then another. I moaned. Then he pulled out, which made me grunt. He snickered. "So eager."

He added a third finger, and right when I was about to come. He replaced it with his cock. He slid in slowly, which felt weird at first, then as he moved, he inserted a finger in my vagina and rubbed my clit. I spasmed right away, and he was pumping into me. I moaned loudly as he bit into my skin. "Kol, fuck!"

A loud banging on the door made us pause. "Lovebirds, time to come out! I'll give you five minutes or I'm coming in there," Amelia sang through the door.

"Go away," Kol grunted as he continued to thrust into me.

"I'm serious. This is important."

"Fuck." He pulled out and sat me on top of him. "Bite me," he whispered.

I bit him as he requested and he moved faster. I felt his fangs on my shoulder, which had me screaming out an orgasm as he grunted out his release.

"I'm going to kill Amelia," Kol growled.

I chuckled as I kissed him. "Good morning. What a way to wake up."

"Are you okay? Do you feel okay?" He gestured behind me.

My face colored. "Yes. That was... wow." I hid a smile, and I caught a grin on his face before I turned to get dressed. Who would have thought Kol was a freaking god in the bedroom?

A pang of guilt hit me. I needed to speak to the princes. However, Kol was also my mate, so I didn't regret enjoying my time with him, but I felt guilty about not talking to my other two mates first. What would I do if they didn't accept Kol? I was so conflicted, but I didn't want to hold back in exploring my relationship with Kol. I felt the bond just as strongly as I did with the princes.

I stepped out of the room with my head buried in the sand—another problem for another day. I couldn't reach my mates anyway, even if I tried.

"Finally." Amelia rolled her eyes, but there was no bite to it. She looked more amused than anything.

"What's up?" Kol asked with his arms crossed.

I moved to sit in front of Amelia, but Kol tugged me closer and wrapped his arms around me and rested his chin on my head.

Amelia watched us for a moment; her lips turned up slightly, but she said nothing. "I have to warn you, the Queen knows about Vi. I don't know how. I think she must have some spies, or we have a traitor in our ranks. Either way, I suggest you tell the King yourself before the Queen makes her move."

"What?" Kol straightened up, and his hold on me tightened. Cold filled my veins, and my stomach dropped.

"Just worry about your father. I got the Queen and the traitor."

"You think it's a traitor?" Kol's icy tone was back.

"I'm hoping it's not, but only the inner circle knows she's here. Aside from her mates, King Rahl, Carlisle, and the headmaster, no one else knows. I checked all of them, and it couldn't be them. It was definitely from someone here."

"If you—"

"Say no more, brother. I know what you want. Trust me. I'm on it."

"You know I trust you, Amie."

She smirked and glanced my way. "You take care of him, you hear?"

I nodded and flashed her a grateful smile. She considered me for a moment, gave me a curt nod, and left. I liked her. She protected Kol as fiercely as a mama bear.

"What are you smiling at?"

"Nothing. I like her."

"Good. Only a handful of people matter to me in this world, and she's one of them. It means a lot to me that you like her." He kissed the top of my head.

"What are you going to do about the Queen or your father?"

"Don't worry about it. I'll protect you. Even if it means that I ascend to the throne, nothing will happen to you. I promise." He pulled me in tightly, as if he was the one who needed reassurance.

Chapter 4

Kol

"FATHER, I WOULD APPRECIATE it if we keep this between us. I don't want anyone to know. Not even the Queen."

"How could you ask me that? You know how vicious she gets. We shouldn't keep secrets from her. It will be worse if she finds out."

Amelia assured me they would preoccupy the Queen for the rest of the afternoon, and she had swept the chamber for any spy devices, so we were safe. I withdrew from my seat and sat closer to my father. His eyes widened in surprise, but it was gone in an instant. I had kept my distance from my father since I moved out of the castle.

I remembered when I was a child, and I would always search his eyes, hoping to see some life behind his gaze—something I had only witnessed a handful of times.

As usual, his dead eyes gazed back at me as if there was no one alive inside of him.

"I need to tell you something important, Father. There is no other way to say it, so I'm just going to tell you. I don't know how much you know about Viola, but she's my mate." I held my breath as I studied his reaction.

His eyes swelled with life. It was like a cloud lifted, and he saw me for the first time in a very long time. His face broke into a genuine smile. I swallowed a lump in my throat since I hadn't seen this look on my father since I was a child.

He leaned over and hugged me. "I'm so happy for you, son. Your mother would be so happy if she were here."

"I know. I wish she were here."

"I do too," he said in a sad tone. "So, tell me more about Viola. Why is she different, and why are we keeping her a secret?"

I hesitated for only a moment, but then I told him everything. I trusted my father.

I used to think he didn't love me since he allowed the evil Queen to abuse me. However, when I got older, I found out that she was a shrewd wench who had kept her cruel ways from him—something Amanda and Deacon had confirmed.

My father got up and paced the room. He paused a few times and opened his mouth to say something, then continued to walk. He was deep in thought, which made me nervous. He didn't look angry. He was more confused and curious if I were to guess.

"I agree. No one should know about her. The Queen will want to meet her, but I will buy us time. I need to check on something first. I will call on you when I know more," he muttered, with hardly a backward glance at me.

My brow rose in shock, and I didn't move, hoping he would return and give me more of an explanation. Then I shook myself from my bewilderment and left the room before the bitch came back.

As I entered the secret passage, Amelia straightened up. "How did it go?"

I chuckled. "Why are you waiting for me?"

"I was worried, you prick," she said as she punched my arm.

"Geez, okay. No need to get violent."

"So?"

"Well... it was weird."

"What do you mean?"

"He took it okay, I think. He hugged me and..."

"That's great!"

"Wait. I'm not done. He asked about Vi. So, I told him everything."

She raised a brow.

"I trust him."

She nodded in agreement.

"Then, he got weird. He started pacing and said he needed to check something out. He said to not tell anyone, and he'll buy us time from the Queen."

She lifted her brows in disbelief. "He actually said that?"

"I know. It's weird, right?"

"Yeah. He usually lets her get away with anything."

"What do you think this means?"

She was silent for a moment, and she said nothing until we reached the command center. Her parents looked up when we entered, and before they opened their mouths to ask how the meeting went, Amelia said, "Don't wait for me. I'm not sure how long I'll be gone. I need to finish my mission. This is big. I have a feeling my intel is tied to what the King is searching for."

I glanced at Deacon and Amanda, but they shared a confused look. I turned around to ask for Amelia to elaborate, but she was gone.

"Do you know what that was about?" I asked.

They both shook their heads. "No. You know her. She wouldn't say anything unless she was absolutely certain," Amanda said.

"Tell us how the meeting went," Deacon added.

I repeated my story.

"That's great." Deacon said.

"I never doubted Henry," Amanda said.

I hid a smile since I knew they were close as friends when my father lived there. I stayed long enough to catch up and chat about what they were working on. I bid them goodbye as they gave me assurances to keep a close eye on the evil Queen and warn me if she made a move.

With nothing else to do, I scurried back to the apartment, eager to spend time with my mate.

I was an idiot for suppressing my feelings. I could have had her sooner, even if I wasn't sure if the Shifter Heirs would have had a problem with our mating. I had long suspected we were all bonded to her somehow, including the Caster heir. Since day one, she drew us to her. Not once did we all come together and work for a common cause, but with Vi, it changed.

When I reached Vi, we basked in each other's company, only coming up for air for necessities.

It had been a couple of days, but there was still no word from my father. I was easing my worry by allowing Vi to distract me. Amelia had also gone missing. The only update we got was from the daily reports on the Shifters' status sent by Deacon and Amanda.

On the third day, I lay awake early in the morning with my arms wrapped around Vi as I slowly traced her soft skin with my fingers. I refused to have her clothed as long as I was around, and she graciously obliged. I gazed down at her perfect body and felt lucky to have her as my mate. She kept up with my insatiable hunger towards her blood and body with no complaints and returned it with equal passion. I don't recall being so happy in my entire existence.

My fingers outlined her nipple, and a soft moan escaped her lips. Her eyes were still closed; she was still asleep. Leaning over, I placed a gentle kiss on my favorite spot on her neck and buried my nose there as I inhaled her scent. My fangs ached, which had me nipping at her skin. My fingers tightened on her hips as I rubbed myself on her ass.

She was like a fucking drug. I couldn't think. All I wanted to do was take her and drink her blood.

I wondered if she would mind if I fucked her right then. Using her wetness, I started prepping her backside. She moaned again. "Baby, you love this, so I'm assuming you're consenting. Tell me to stop if you don't want it, okay?"

She said nothing, but continued to moan. As soon as she was ready, I slid inside of her. She gasped, and her eyes opened. "Kol. I thought I was dreaming," she panted.

I paused. "Do you want me to stop?"

"No, baby. It feels so good. You have my permission to wake me up."

"Oh, you asked for it."

"Shut up and go faster."

I did as my mate asked, as I felt her build-up. Then I heard the door open, and I vaguely saw Amelia, so I ignored her. We were both so close, so I moved faster and added my finger, and soon, Vi was yelling my name and drawing me to the edge with her.

"Goddammit, don't you two have any shame? This is an emergency!"

I fell on top of Vi and lifted my head to glance at Amelia. "You're the one who barged into my room without knocking."

"Yes. Well, as I said, it's an emergency. Get dressed, you two. Now."

I sighed and placed a kiss on Vi's neck. "Sorry about her. I was far from done. I wanted to drink your blood for our second round."

She giggled and got up.

Once we were showered and dressed, we met a glaring Amelia in the living room.

"Didn't I say it was an emergency?"

"We didn't fuck in the shower, so we were out here as fast as possible," I argued.

Vi looked mortified.

Amelia had her hands on her hips with her eyes narrowed, looking like she was contemplating where to stab me.

"Sorry, Amelia," Vi said.

"What is it?" I asked as I pulled Vi to sit on my lap on the sofa.

"I found our spy."

"I hardly think that's an emergency for you to barge into my room for!"

"Let me finish!" She scowled.

I raised my hands in apology.

She glared, making sure I didn't interrupt before she continued. "The spy was the last piece of my mission. After that, I am now one hundred percent certain how far back the Queen's involvement is with the Casters." She was speaking fast without looking at me. This must be huge, so I got up and stopped in front of Amelia.

"Tell me."

"Kol. She knows about Vi. She's known for a while, and she just lacked an excuse to get to her. Since her last attack, we had fortified the tower, so they couldn't get in, even with the spy. So she needed to manipulate the King to agree to side with the Casters since they couldn't afford to attack the castle outright. Doing that would have been suicide since they would fight two wars, and they don't have the manpower to do that."

I shook her shoulders gently. "Amie, you're rambling. Get to the point."

She finally met my eyes and stared at me with guilt and sorrow. Dread filled the pit of my stomach, suddenly not wishing to hear what she had to say.

"I'm sorry, Kol, but she killed your mom." She laid her hand on my arm, but I stiffened in shock. Coldness ran down my spine, permeating my whole body, then my chest tightened. Heat quickly replaced the cold, and I knew my eyes were red.

"Kol. Listen to me. Do nothing stupid. We need to do this the right way. If you want to take her down once and for all, we need to...."

I sidestepped her, not wanting to hear what she had to say, and proceeded to the door.

"Vi. Help!" I vaguely heard her scream.

I stepped out, but something blurred in front of me, and I momentarily forgot my rage as Vi stood in front of the door.

"Kol. Listen to Amelia. You need to calm down."

I blinked at my mate, but the bitch Queen was still alive, killed my mother, and threatened my mate. No. She needed to die. I needed to protect Vi.

"Amelia, be ready," I heard Vi say but didn't understand it, so I ignored her as I moved her aside, ensuring I didn't hurt her.

"Kol. Don't make me do this. I don't want to hurt you," Vi warned, but she wasn't making any sense, so I continued to move past her.

"Okay. Don't say I didn't warn you." I heard behind me as I strode away. Someone tackled me from behind and pinned me to the ground. I struggled, but whoever it was freakishly strong. She had my hands behind my back and had her weight on me. I was getting pissed, so I twisted to break the hold, but I couldn't do it. "Calm down, Kol," Vi murmured in my ear.

Vi's voice startled me, which cleared my head, so I leaned my face on the floor and took deep breaths.

"Are you calm?"

I nodded.

"If I let you go, will you go back inside?"

I nodded.

"Did I hurt you?"

I shook my head.

She kissed my cheek and leaped off me.

I got up slowly since my muscle ached from the struggle.

I glanced at Amelia, who was laughing her ass off. "If it wasn't for the seriousness of the situation," she said as she continued to laugh, "I would have taken a video of that. I can't believe your mate can kick your ass."

I glowered at her.

"Sorry. I know now is not the time. I will tease you about it later."

I shook my head in response and walked inside the room.

Amelia followed with a serious expression. "I'm sorry, Kol. I didn't mean to be insensitive to your mother...."

"It's not that," I snapped.

"What is it then?"

Vi sat on the single sofa. I tugged on her hand, pulling her to my lap as my arms wrapped around her waist. I inhaled her scent, which helped lower my heart rate. "That bitch has been tormenting me since I was a child. Ever since I grew stronger, I've been itching to take her down, but I didn't want to take on my father. Now, I have a reason. It's a disgrace for her to sit on my mother's throne."

Vi caressed my arm while Amelia finally sat in front of us with a troubled look on her face. "I know that, Kol. It was why I was cautious about gathering this information. It took me years to finally get it. Now is not the time to be hasty. If you march in there and accuse her, she will deny it. We need iron-clad information to present to the King."

"I don't need information. I can take her," I said firmly.

"What would you do if your father took her side? Will you take on your father too?"

My lips thinned, hating when Amelia was right.

"I suspect you are getting stronger. Perhaps you're even strong enough to take him on, but will your conscience allow you to do it?" she continued.

"Okay. I get your point." I glared at her. "What do you suggest we do then?"

She flashed me a mischievous smile. "We bait her."

Chapter 5

Vi

"HOW DO I LOOK?" I ASKED Kol for maybe the third time. I smoothed the skirt of the simple dress Amelia bought me. It was dark red with light material, matched with flats, so it would be easy for me to fight if needed.

"You look beautiful," Kol said distractedly. He had been busy planning every detail of this day with Amelia and her parents for the past two nights. He would crawl into bed exhausted and wake up early, rushing out the door. The only time he stopped was when I made him. Otherwise, he wouldn't feed. He needed his strength if we were to fight today.

"Are you ready?" he asked.

"As ready as I'll ever be."

He pulled my hips close and peered into my eyes, his fingers twirling the gentle curls in my hair. "When this is all over. I want to lock you inside my room and take my time with you before I have to share you with your other mates," he said, and kissed me. "I'm not worried since I know you can take care of yourself, but please promise me you won't do anything reckless."

"I promise," I said.

He clasped my hand and led me to the throne room, accompanied by Amelia and the elite guards. We marched in silence with nervous anticipation thick in the air.

The King and Queen sat in their thrones. My eyes darted, fixing on the King, who looked like Kol except for his eyes, which were darker. The King stared back at me. His eyes hadn't left me since I walked into the room. I shifted my weight and peeked at the Queen, who sat with her back straight, penetrating eyes darting between Kol and me.

"Father, Queen. This is Viola, my mate." Kol bowed.

"Your Majesties." I curtsied.

"Pleased to meet you, Viola," the King said. His eyes bore into me as he inspected me.

My hands itched to fidget, so I clutched Kol's hands tightly. God, he probably hated me as well. Why was he staring at me as if he'd seen a ghost?

The Queen wore a displeased look on her face as she looked down on us. Amelia shifted her weight next to me, which didn't help my nervousness.

Finally, the Queen stood and walked closer. "So you are who the fuss is about," she murmured when she stood less than a foot in front of me. Kol's hand tightened in mine in response.

"What was that?" Kol asked.

"Oh, nothing," she said.

The King blurred to her side, which startled everyone, including the Queen. "Oh, Henry. You scared me." She giggled as she laid her hand on his chest.

The King stepped to the side to dislodge her touch, which brought him in front of me. "Doesn't she remind you of someone?" he asked as he tilted his head, scanning me like I was an interesting specimen.

Her gaze snapped to the King, and her eyes narrowed. "Of course not. She has a plain face. Why don't we get on with this? We have other matters to attend to." She laid her hand on his arm again, but he shook it off.

"No. I insist you look closely and tell me if she reminds you of anyone, Delia," he said in a soft tone but with a hint of danger.

Her eyes grew. I glanced at Kol, who had a look of surprise on his face.

"I... I don't know," she stammered, which seemed uncharacteristic of the Queen.

"You see, Delia. Her eyes are like her mother's, but her face." He smiled. "It's just like her father's."

I sucked in a breath and froze as I stared into the King. What? The King held my gaze for another moment, then turned to the Queen. "Don't you agree?"

The Queen's face looked ashen. Her eyes were darting around the room as if she was ready to bolt. Her weight shifted, then the King's hand moved too fast for me to see, and as if in slow motion, she looked down to her chest. My gaze followed hers, and buried in her chest was the King's hand.

Kol pulled my waist closer to him as we watched the horror scene before us.

"Tell me the truth, Delia, or I will prolong your pain. Tell me who she looks like?"

"Henry, please," she choked. Blood dripped from the side of her mouth.

The King squeezed, and she gasped in pain. She clutched the King's hands with both of hers with her claws extended, but it didn't bother the King. "She... She looks like Bea and... and Dante."

Kol gasped. My eyes darted from Kol, the King, and then the Queen, wondering who Bea and Dante were.

"Now, tell me what happened to Dante."

"I swear, I don't know. I had nothing to do..." she choked on her words and gasped in some air.

"I promise. I don't..."

"Fine. Tell me about the night my mate, Elena, died."

"Please. Henry."

The King's eyes turned red, and he squeezed harder. The Queen choked, and blood gushed out of her mouth, soaking the front of her in red.

"Tell me," he hissed.

"The Casters gave me a spelled knife. Someone helped me bypass your wards as several of them attacked your men." She coughed and took a shallow breath in. "Then, when the halls were clear, I knocked on your door, and Elena answered. I taunted her with Kol's life and stabbed her with the knife."

Henry's hand twitched as if he was about to yank her heart out of her chest. Then he released her, and she fell to the ground, gasping in lungfuls of air.

"Get me Adrian and Larsen." His voice boomed. Two Vampires appeared behind Dalia, who was still gasping on the floor. "Get her up," the King commanded.

Dalia's legs buckled, and her eyes looked terrified. The King slapped her face so hard that I heard bones crack. Her head flopped to the side, which made me think she was dead, but then Henry grabbed her chin, and her eyes fluttered. In a low voice, he said, "I'm not done with you yet. You will suffer for what you have done to my family and me."

There was a whimpering, gurgling sound at the back of her throat.

"Take her to the dungeon. Make sure it's spelled. I want twenty-four-seven surveillance on her."

Amelia stepped up and bowed low. "Your majesty. I beg your pardon. I have strong intel that several guards and others are loyal to the Queen and the Casters. I volunteer to personally escort her along with my men until we clean house."

"You're Amanda and Deacon's daughter?"

"Yes, Your Majesty."

"Granted. That's a good idea. We shall talk some more once I'm done here."

Henry took several unsteady breaths in and out as Kol and I were rooted on the spot and didn't dare move. Finally, he turned to us, walked to Kol, and pulled him into a hug. My eyes stung with unshed tears as I shared their pain for Elena.

Once he released Kol, he turned to me and said, "Viola, give me time to gather myself and get cleaned up. I'll meet you in the receiving room."

I nodded my head mechanically, still lost for words. He blurred out of the room, and I let out a nervous breath and glanced at Kol, who looked lost. I pulled him into a hug and whispered, "Are you okay?"

"I am now."

He grabbed my hand and led me to the King's private receiving room but didn't elaborate further. I was too lost with my thoughts to pry until the King joined us.

"I apologize that you had to witness that, Viola."

"No need to apologize, Your Majesty," I said, remembering my manners, even though my nerves were buzzing to get information.

"Please, call me Henry. It was what your parents called me."

This was it. I had been searching for a long time to find out where I came from, and now I'd finally gotten some answers. I glanced at Kol, who wore a confused expression, which made my chest tighten in fear. What if I didn't like what I heard?

Henry got up and poured himself a glass of whiskey. "Does the tower still have a bar?" he asked Kol.

"No. It doesn't," Kol responded.

He snickered and took a sip of the drink, then sat on the sofa. "The bar was Dante's request, while I wanted leather couches. We built the tower to get away from my crazy father. We had designed the tower for years but couldn't find an adequate reason to convince the sadistic King to allow us to live off the castle." He tipped the glass and gulped down the rest of the contents.

"I got it, Father." Kol got up and brought the whole decanter to him.

He nodded and poured some more into his glass. "When I met your mother, the King finally allowed us to build the tower. Dante is my cousin, but he was like a brother to me. I was lucky that my mate and my brother got along. For a while, life was perfect, especially when he met your mother." He had a far-away look and didn't speak for a while. "Elena was unhappy. She grew up as a commoner and hated the castle life. I was worried she would leave me. Then, one night, Dante convinced me to raid a Casters' lab who were doing experiments on supernaturals." He gazed at me with sorrow in his eyes. "It was there that he rescued your mother, Bea. The Casters had been experimenting on her for a couple of years, trying to breed a hybrid. However, none of their victims lived long enough to achieve their goal. Your mother was the only survivor, because she was a Shifter Heir."

"What?" My hand flew to my mouth. My mother was tortured and experimented on... I couldn't wrap my mind around that, so I focused on the fact that Rahl might be my family. If he... oh, God. A dreadful feeling sank into my stomach.

"Yes. Rahl is also your family."

My face paled as I stared at Kol in horror. Henry chuckled. "I know what you're thinking. The supernaturals aren't like humans, and we don't have issues with DNA interbreeding. Many of us marry our cousins, but to make you feel better, your mates are your distant cousins. Even though human sentimentality was only implemented in the modern ages since inter-family breeding was widely practiced in the olden ages, only in the immediate family was there such an issue with DNA dilution and maybe first cousins. It is even legal to marry second cousins all over the world in modern times."

It took me a moment to think about what he said. He was right; I didn't recall a lot of my classmates who were close to their distant cousins. It wasn't the same as the immediate family. Although, it made me slightly uncomfortable—perhaps it was my human upbringing.

"I digress. When Dante met Bea, it surprised us to realize that they were mates since she was a Shifter and we were Vampires. However, from the experiments done to Bea, the

Casters succeeded in changing her DNA. It was something we couldn't explain, but it was also something they couldn't fight. They were mates, and they were happy. Having Bea around also made Elana happy, which led to conceiving Kol." He flashed a warm smile at Kol. "It was the happiest I've seen your mother." He paused, and his features morphed into something calm. "Then Bea got pregnant. They experimented on her and tried for two years, but nothing worked. Then suddenly, she was pregnant with a Vampire baby. It should have been impossible since interspecies breeding was unheard of. Our DNA is incompatible. We knew if anyone found out, the Casters would take you, so Dante and Bea went into hiding. You heard what happened to Elena." He finished the rest of his drink and leaned back heavily on the seat. "Soon after Elena died, my father forced me into a marriage with that evil bitch. I searched for Bea and heard she died in childbirth, along with the baby. Then I also heard that Dante tried to avenge his family's death and died in combat. In just a few short months, I lost everything—everyone I loved." He closed his eyes and didn't speak for a long time.

"I would have followed them, but I had you." He gazed at Kol without lifting his head. "I knew I hadn't been much of a father. In fact, I've probably been a horrible father, but everything in me died with your mother and Dante. I'm only alive because of you. I couldn't bear to leave you, and I promised your mother that I wouldn't let anything happen to you." He straightened up and reached over to squeeze Kol's leg.

Kohl leaned forward once again, and they hugged.

My parents were dead, but I had Rahl and Henry. I still couldn't believe I was a hybrid. I'd been searching for my past, and now I finally knew what I was. It all came down to the Casters, and they were the reason for all this pain.

"Thank you for telling me about my past. I had been searching for my parents since I'd been introduced to the supernatural world. I'm sorry I brought on this terrible loss to your family. If it weren't for my existence, you wouldn't be going through it."

"Don't say that, Viola. There is no one to blame but the Casters and Delia. She was always jealous and would have found another way. The Casters used her hatred as an opportunity."

"Thank you for saying that."

"What should we do? They're still after her," Kol said.

"I will set up a meeting with Rahl. It's about time he knew the truth, and it's also time to end the corrupt reign of Lucille Pruitt. She is the reason for so much pain and suffering."

"Thank you, Father. Let me get Vi safely back in the tower, and I will come and help."

"I would appreciate that, son. You'll find me in the dungeons. We will need Amanda and Deacon's help." We stood, and Henry gave me a hug, which I returned.

"Thank you again for telling me about my past."

"You're welcome. I'm glad to have you in my family. It's like I have a piece of them back. When I look at Kol, I see Elena's eyes. When I see you, I see Bea and Dante." He smiled and kissed me on the forehead.

Chapter 6

Kol

IT WAS THREE IN THE morning. I felt drained, but I was also craving Vi. I watched her at the foot of the bed, admiring that she wore my shirt and boxer shorts to sleep, then stripped off my clothes and crawled into bed as I trailed kisses up her leg and on her stomach. I loved that she was a deep sleeper but still so responsive. I should have let her sleep, but I needed her. I feasted on her breasts as I stripped her bottoms off. She ran her fingers through my hair, so I knew she was awake. I kissed down between her legs, and her moans cut through the still of the night. As soon as I milked out her first orgasm, I was inside of her, ripping the shirt off and piercing her flesh with my fangs. Drinking from her made sex more intense. Her blood tasted marvelous.

One taste of her blood and body, and I couldn't get enough. I had to take her until we were both too exhausted to continue. Usually, by the time we were done, her flesh would be peppered with bite marks. I wanted to share the feeling with her, so I said, "Baby, I want you to bite me." She studied me to make sure I was serious. "Use your mimic powers and suck my blood like a Vampire."

"I've never done that before. I mean, when I claimed you all as my mates, I didn't drink your blood."

"Now's the time to practice," I murmured against her skin. "Bite me," I repeated as I continued to thrust in and out. I allowed my fangs to extend, which she copied, and I bit into her flesh. Soon, I felt her fangs sinking into my neck.

Euphoria filled my veins. "That's it, baby. Keep doing that. Yes." The feeling built, and my whole body tensed. Without my control, I climaxed before she was done licking my wounds shut. "Holy shit. That felt amazing." I exhaled, catching my breath. My limbs shuddered as my body came down from the intense experience.

"Wow, that was... I didn't think I would like the taste of blood, but I kinda liked yours," she said with flushed cheeks.

"I felt your venom seep into my skin, so the bond is both ways now." I beamed. "Just don't bite anyone else."

"Don't worry. I don't like the thought of another's blood in my mouth."

I smiled in satisfaction, but the rising sun peeking through the clouds caught my attention. "I want to spend all day with you so you can practice drinking from me. However, we only have a few hours left before I have to share you."

"What do you mean?"

"Never mind that. Remember to bite into me at the end. But only at the end. Okay?"

She nodded as I continued to kiss her neck. I'd had little rest, but I didn't waste our last night sleeping. So, we spent the remaining few hours owning each other's bodies.

Vi grew more insatiable for my blood as the blood bond got stronger. As I was recovering, she bit into my chest and had me coming without sex. It shocked me to know her bite could elicit such a reaction from me. I never thought I would want another's bite as much.

Our blood bond was nothing like our mate bond. However, it enhanced our lovemaking and made every touch and every bite more intense. Being with Vi gave me a high that no drug could come close to.

I must have gotten an hour of sleep, but I had to get up and meet with the shifters and my father, so with difficulty, I left Vi naked under the sheets.

Rubbing my tired eyes, I listened as my father and King Rahl discussed their alliance against the Casters. It had been a couple of hours since Father had announced to King Rahl that he was declaring war against them, but he had mentioned nothing yet about Vi and her mother's history. I supposed he would tell him in private. The kings had their heads bowed together with no sign of ending their conversation any time soon, so I pulled the princes aside. "I need to speak with you two about Vi." I gestured for them to follow me into the next room.

"How is she?" Tristan asked.

"Where is she?" Sebastian crossed his arms.

"I wanted to speak with you before I took you to her. This should come from me."

"What did you do, bloodsucker?" Tristan stood next to his brother and scowled.

"If you let me finish, I can explain," I said steadily. "Vi is okay. She's more than okay. I'm speaking to you first as a courtesy since we all need to get along if we want this to work out."

"What the fuck are you talking about?" Seb snapped, while Tristan continued to glower.

"Jesus, are you two always like this?" I took a deep breath as they were trying my patience. "What I'm trying to say, if you let me, is that Vi and I are mates."

Tristan's fist came up, but I dodged his punch. "What the fuck?"

"What did you do?" Sebastian asked.

"I was trying to do this the right way since Vi felt really guilty that she couldn't talk to you first before we bonded, but since you two are being dicks, then go ahead and waste your reunion fighting." I stormed out of the room.

"Wait," one of them called out.

"Were you serious?" Tristan asked.

"Yes. We're mated, and I suspect Carlisle will be next. So get used to the idea and stop being a jealous prick."

They both stared at me in shock.

"I'll let you two stew on that information. Once you're ready, I'll take you to her," I called over my shoulder and slammed the door.

Those two needed to get their heads straight, or I would kick their asses. I didn't want them upsetting Vi. I surely wouldn't take them to her until they accepted this. I considered going back into the chamber and standing by my father, but I strode instead to the tech room.

"Hi, Kol," Amanda said.

"Is Amelia here?"

"No. We received a message that she's guarding the Queen," Deacon answered.

I snickered. "Why am I not surprised? I hope she took her men with her."

"Yes. They're good men. They don't let her out of their sight." Amanda chuckled.

"Good. Keep me updated on the Queen's status, will you?"

"Of course," Deacon said.

I hung out for a bit longer until, finally, I got a message from Tristan.

Surprisingly, it only took them a couple of hours and about a dozen questions before they warmed up to the idea.

This was better than I expected. Perhaps we would learn to get along after all.

Chapter 7

Vi

"HMM, KOL. DON'T YOU ever get tired?" I mumbled as I snuggled up to his warmth, which felt different since Kol had little body heat. I woke up more since I also felt kisses on my shoulders and hands on my breasts. *Why did it feel like there were extra mouths and hands? Was I dreaming?*

My eyes snapped open, and I sucked in a breath to see two naked Shifter heirs next to me. Tears burst out of me as I grabbed onto them and hugged them close. "Oh my God. Am I dreaming? I've been so worried about you two. I can't believe you're here."

"I'm sorry it took us so long to get back to you." Tristan captured my mouth in a bruising kiss, followed by Sebastian, who languidly kissed my lips, taking his time, savoring every stroke.

"I missed you," he murmured.

"I missed you too."

"We were going crazy not being around you. We almost risked it all and snuck in here just to hold you," Sebastian said.

"I love you, Vi," Tristan whispered as he kissed my neck.

"I love you too. How's Rahl? What's going on with...?"

"Shhh..." Sebastian flicked his tongue on my nipple as his fingers slid between my legs. "You have no idea how much I've dreamt of this."

"Yeah, I was tired of my hand." Tristan laughed.

I giggled, but then they both slid fingers inside me at both ends, which caught my breath.

"I need to be inside you, Vi," Sebastian whispered.

"But..."

"Don't worry. We'll make sure you're ready for both of us first," Tristan said as he continued.

I wanted to protest and ask how Rahl was doing, but their touches quickly filled me with desire. I needed them just as much as they needed me.

I needed to feel them and make sure they were real.

Sebastian replaced his fingers with his mouth as Tristan continued to prep my behind. The sensation was too much, which had me pulling and pushing them at the same time. My breathing was strained, and my eyes rolled back from the intensity of their touch. When I couldn't hold it anymore, I screamed out their names as my body spasmed in release, but they didn't stop. They continued until my limbs were shaking, and the ache to be filled had my body writhing. "Please..." I panted.

Sebastian thrust inside me, which satiated the ache he created. Tristan quickly followed, and I leaned my head on his shoulders as I adjusted to their size. My hips rocked, and they followed. It took them a moment to get into a rhythm, but an explosive orgasm hit me when they did. They both rocked faster, which had me peaking again. Loud moans escaped me, and I clawed whichever arm I could reach as I felt like I would die from the blissful sensation until finally, another release hit me, which Sebastian quickly followed. Then, soon after, so did Tristan.

I fell on Sebastian's chest with my eyes closed. Could someone die from too much sex?

The princes peppered me with kisses and laid me on the bed, but I was spent and too exhausted. As soon as my head hit the pillow, my eyes were heavy with sleep.

I woke up to an empty bed, which had my heart contracting in panic. I quickly showered and changed. I feared I had imagined the princes with me, so I almost ran out of the shower before rinsing off. I didn't think I would survive it if I lost another loved one. My nerves didn't settle until I spotted my three mates deep in conversation. My lips turned upward as I watched them lean toward each other as they whispered in what looked like a serious discussion.

Something inside of me settled; ever since I had lost my mother, this was the first time I felt like I'd found my home. However, a nagging feeling had my brows drawing together. It felt as if something was missing—like a last piece of the puzzle. I brushed it off because we were new and we weren't home. This was Kol's home and not Tristan or Sebastian's. Or maybe it was something else that I couldn't put my finger on. Either way, I would fight like hell to keep my guys. Those selfish Casters wouldn't know what hit them if they ever threatened one of them.

I straightened up as I remembered Carlisle. He was at their mercy. What if he was hurt and that sadistic bitch Lucille tortured him to get to me?

"Hey, love. What's the matter?" Kol cupped my face to get my attention.

"What if she has Carlisle?" I said in a low voice, not wanting to say it out loud in fear of it coming true.

Tristan tugged on my hand and led me to the sofa, then sat me on his lap. "I promise he's fine."

Sebastian kissed my shoulder as he sat next to us. "We've kept in touch, and he's been busy recruiting other Casters to join his coven against this war."

"Oh, God. He's making himself a target." Tears welled in my eyes, and I moved to get up, but Tristan kept his arms wrapped around me, trapping me on his lap.

Kol sat on the coffee table and grabbed my hand. "Vi, listen to me. We have a system in place. If one of us is in trouble, we are instructed to reach out to the others for backup. We also check in with each other daily. I promise he is safe."

I held his gaze, and all I saw was certainty in his words, so I nodded. I felt the princes relax next to me, and Tristan pressed a kiss on my temple.

Sebastian tugged on me, so I sat between them and he held on to my hand while Tristan took the other. I smiled at them, but then I sat up and dislodged their hold when I gazed up at Kol. Tristan tried pulling on my hand again, but I got up and stood far away from the three of them.

"What's wrong, Vi?" Sebastian asked.

"I guess we should talk about... this." I made a circle, gesturing to all of us. I felt my face burning in embarrassment. "I mean... it's just... I don't want it to be awkward. You know?" I wrapped my arms around myself and shifted my weight.

Sebastian stood and took a step towards me, but I held a hand up to stop him. His face fell, which filled me with guilt, but I couldn't show favoritism and hurt one while I was with the others. We needed to establish rules and expectations.

"Before we move forward, I just wanted to talk about us." I hesitated since I still couldn't wrap my mind around the fact that I had all three prince heirs as my mates. *What does that mean? Didn't their race depend on them to populate? Because I sure as hell am not sharing.* The thought of another touching one of them gave me murderous thoughts.

"Vi, honey. You look angry. What's going on?" Tristan stood next to Seb. They both looked like they wanted to launch themselves at me, and they kept sending dirty glances at Kol, while Kol wore a blank expression.

"I just feel like we need to discuss our situation."

"What did you want to talk about?" Sebastian asked.

"I mean, is everyone okay with..." I peered at Kol, whose eyes flashed red, so I hurriedly added, "I mean, how is everyone dealing with the multiple mate thing?" I finished lamely.

How did one talk about this shit? I couldn't bring myself to say, *how do you feel about sharing me?* It felt naughty and conceited. Not to mention presumptuous. *What if they don't want to share? What if they want me to choose? Oh, no.*

"Vi. You're doing it again," Tristan said.

"What?"

"Look, whatever is going on in that pretty little head of yours, it's not the case." Tristan took a step forward, but I wasn't ready, so I took a step back. His eyes tightened, but he kept a neutral expression.

"What do you mean?"

"We've discussed our situation." Sebastian took a step next to Tristan. "Although we've had our differences, we're willing to put those aside for you." I stared at the Shifter heirs with a frown, still not completely understanding what they were trying to convey.

"Kol, tell her, will you?" Tristan snapped.

Kol's intense eyes hadn't left me. It took him a moment, but eventually, he stood and stepped next to Sebastian. "Vi, do you have a problem with our situation?"

I shook my head.

"Are you having any regrets?" His gorgeous green eyes were back, but his whole body was still tense.

I shook my head, and his shoulders relaxed, then his mouth twitched into a smile. "Vi, I know you're new to our world, so let me explain something to you. As your mates, we are here to worship you and give you everything you desire." He closed the gap between us and pulled my waist closer. Tristan and Sebastian stepped in behind me, their chests pressing in on me. "We know this is unconventional since we're all from different races, but there's no denying we're all mated, which is sacred to all supernaturals. So, even if we've had our differences in the past, that was in the past the moment we sealed the bond. You come first." Kol pressed his lips to mine. I wanted to drape my arms around his neck, but they caged me in. However, I felt Tristan and Sebastian's lips on my neck and shoulders, which had my veins buzzing with desire.

"It's just a little weird," I said in a small voice. "I don't want to show favoritism, and I don't want to leave anyone out. I want all three of you equally, so please don't ask me to choose. I can't."

Tristan spun me around. "Honey, we will never do that. We know that would make you unhappy. As Kol said, our bond is sacred. Ever since we've mated, my world shifted. My only purpose is to make sure you're safe and happy." He pulled my hips closer and pressed his mouth to mine. I was breathless when he released me.

I drew in a stuttered breath. "Is it selfish of me to not want to share any of you with others?" I asked without meeting their eyes.

Now it was Sebastian's turn to pull me to his chest. "Vi, aren't you listening? We don't want anyone else. We only want you. I know you grew up as a human, but it's different for supernaturals. Once bonded, your entire world changes. Tell me, are you attracted to any other guys?"

My brow furrowed. Then my stomach fell. I wanted to push away, but they still had me caged in.

"What is it?" Seb asked.

"I..."

"Just tell us, Vi," Tristan whispered. His lips were tickling my neck.

"Don't be afraid," Kol said.

"I would like to say no, but... I think I might be a tiny bit attracted to Carlisle." My hands covered my face in embarrassment. Yes, I was officially a greedy slut.

Tristan chuckled as he licked my neck.

"I told you," Kol said.

Sebastian gently pried my hands away from my face. "Vi, we already expected that he might be your fourth mate."

"What?" My eyes grew wide.

Tristan continued to trace my neck and shoulder with his slightly distracting lips. Then Kol leaned down and started kissing the other side of my neck. Sebastian must have noticed my distraction since he pulled our hips even closer and rubbed his growing erection into my stomach. Goosebumps traveled down my spine as I grasped Sebastian's arms. The three of them on me at the same time were wreaking havoc on my senses. "

"H...how... how did you know?" I breathed.

I felt the cold hit my nipples and was surprised to see myself completely naked. Jesus, I was so lost to their touch I didn't even feel my clothes come off. I could no longer keep track of whose lips and hands were whose, but when I felt multiple assaults on my body, my legs buckled. I didn't fall as I was pinned to their bodies, unable to move. The three dominating heirs were too preoccupied torturing my body.

"Oh, God, yes," I said in between loud moans. I closed my eyes and completely let go. It was overwhelming trying to keep track of what they were doing. "Yes. Please. Yes."

They were prolonging my torture. I wanted to come ages ago, but once I came close, someone stopped and changed position. Finally, I felt Kol's fangs sink into my neck, and I let out a shuddering scream as my legs quivered.

After a few heartbeats, I opened my eyes to find Tristan and Sebastian thoroughly flushed and staring down at me with adoring eyes. I shifted and found Kol with the same look. Each of them, fully clothed, still had me caged.

"I love watching you come." Sebastian leaned in close and kissed me.

"That was freaking hot." Tristan grinned and passed me to Kol.

"They're right. You're beautiful," Kol whispered and kissed my neck, walking me to the sofa.

I should have been embarrassed since I was the only one naked, but I wasn't. They made me feel special. "Are you sure everyone is okay with this?"

"Yes," they said in unison.

"We're all grown adults, Vi. If someone has a problem, we can voice it. We all want to get along and make this work." Sebastian grabbed my legs and draped them on his lap.

"What about Carlisle?"

"When you decide to add him to our group, that's your decision," Tristan said, sitting on the coffee table. Kol continued to hold me and twirled my hair in his fingers.

"Um, are you three... did you need... did you want me to take care of...." I flushed.

The bastards snickered.

"We'll have plenty of time to collect. This is all for you," Kol said.

I buried my head in his chest in embarrassment, which prompted more chuckles.

"If I were you, Vi, I would collect some more because when it's our turn, you won't be able to stand," Tristan taunted.

"Hilarious."

"How many times do you think we can make her come?" Tristan asked the guys. I moved to get up, but Kol and Sebastian tightened their hold on me.

My heart sped up, but my belly warmed in anticipation. "Hmm... see that. I think our little minx is game," Tristan continued.

I would get back at the fucker later, or maybe thank him; I couldn't decide yet. Sebastian moved from rubbing my feet to trace long strokes up and down my inner thigh, while Kol traced circles around my breasts.

"The better question is, what are the different ways we can make her come?" Sebastian moved his fingers between my legs. I drew in a ragged breath and dropped my head on Kol's chest. Tristan moved closer and pulled my hip, so it was hanging off the couch. He started stimulating my behind when a loud knocking had all of us freezing. I closed my eyes and took a steadying breath as I closed my legs. *What a freaking cockblock.*

In the blink of an eye, Kol blurred into the room and was handing me a change of clothes. I took them without argument and stepped out of the room as soon as I was sure I was presentable.

My embarrassment flooded out of me from the look on Rahl's face. I just knew that King Henry had told him about my birth mother.

I ran to him and wrapped my arms around his waist. He held me for a long time as tears fell from both of us. When he let go, he cupped my face with his massive hands. "I knew you were special from the moment I laid eyes on you." He looked down with a watery smile. "I felt a connection towards you I couldn't explain. I thought it was the Alpha blood, but it was so much more—you're family. I was right. From the very beginning, I knew," he whispered the last part.

Tears continued to fall, so I buried my face in his chest once more. His words meant more to me than he realized. I knew he adopted me, or I had adopted him as my substitute dad, but to find out that we were actually related and that I wasn't alone meant the world to me. My mates were different. Rahl was family, which was just as important to me. Now, I had two—him and Henry.

Chapter 8

Vi

MR. WILSON LED US TO an enormous suite in the main castle. "I was given strict instructions from King Rahl and King Henry to keep you all in the same room. It took a lot of back and forth to figure out where to house all of you since..." He trailed and cleared his throat. "We worked overtime. Of course, with ample funding from the royals, we transformed the staff tower into an apartment. Although, you all are staying in the staff wing. You're still separated, so you won't need to worry about bumping into the staff. I will make an announcement today that the royals are taking extra precautions to house the heirs in a different location."

I looked around and found a somewhat similar setting as Kol's apartment. "Your staff already sent your belongings, and everything should be in order. As usual, you know where to find me if you need anything."

"Thank you, Mr. Wilson." I smiled.

"Thank you," the princes said distractedly as they studied the suite.

Kol walked the dean to the door as they murmured to each other.

Tristan tugged on my hand as we entered the main room, bypassing the white sofa, the dining table, and the kitchen. My feet froze just a few steps into the threshold. Dominating the space was the most enormous bed I had ever seen. It could fit all four of us with plenty of room to spare. It was like a double super-sized four-poster bed.

"Oh my God. How embarrassing. Who set this up?"

Someone chuckled behind me, and Sebastian kissed my cheeks and strutted into the room, not at all bothered by it.

Kol stood in front of me with his brows furrowed. "What's wrong?" he asked me, but he watched Tristan, who lounged on the ungodly bed, which made me flush even more as Kol asked. "What did you two do now?"

"What made you think we did something?" Sebastian shot back.

Regardless of their reassurance, they haven't stopped bickering. The only time they agreed was with my safety and in the bedroom.

"Then what's—"

"It's the bed." I waved my hands wildly to the horror in front of me. "It's embarrassing. How did they know?"

"Rahl and Father know?" Kol asked in confusion.

I rolled my eyes. Everyone was on a first-name basis, sans titles. They claimed that, through me, they were all related. No one seemed to be bothered that we were distant cousins. I knew we weren't human, so it didn't count, but shouldn't they be weirded out? Just a bit?

I had no regrets, but I was expecting some pushback from someone. Not necessarily my mates, but others. My initial reaction was to brace myself for judgment, and when I didn't get it, it freaked me out.

Rahl and I got little time together. He spent most of his time dominated by the heirs, talking about how to get me back on campus safely and how to get Carlisle, while I spent the entire time wringing my hands, worried that Rahl was saving his lecture since I was sure he would disagree with my mating with his heirs, plus, I had mated with his enemy. However, he said nothing. He left with another long hug and a promise that he would tell me everything I wanted to know about my mom when the war died down.

"So, they arranged this with the dean?" I asked incredulously.

"What's the big deal?" Sebastian asked as Tristan laughed at my discomfort.

"Viola, are you embarrassed by your mates?" Kol's eyes narrowed.

My eyes grew in surprise. "No. I mean... No. I'm damn lucky to have not one but three gorgeous and amazing mates. I just don't want the entire world to know what I do behind closed doors, that's all." I crossed my arms.

"Kol, bring her cute butt over here," Tristan said.

"Wait. Stop." I stepped back, but Kol was too fast for me.

He laid me in between him and Tristan, while Sebastian stood at the foot of the bed.

"Do you know what we can do with an enormous bed?" Tristan murmured as he traced my nipple through my shirt. Kol did the same. At the same time, Sebastian ran his finger along the inner part of my thigh.

I shook my head as my chest rose and fell in heavy pants.

"We can all sleep in the same room and not have to argue about who is sleeping with you. And if you finally decide to add Carlisle, we have plenty of room," Tristan said as he renewed his attention on my breast.

"Most importantly, we have plenty of room to do what we want to do to you." Kol ripped my shirt and bra.

"You have got to stop doing that. I'm running out of clothes."

"We'll buy you more," he said as he popped a nipple in his mouth. Then I felt Sebastian strip me of my shorts.

"Next time, I would like to tie you to the post and blindfold you," Kol whispered as he nipped on my skin with his fangs. I shivered in anticipation. His bite had become one of my favorite things in bed.

Tristan and Sebastian stopped what they were doing, which made me growl. They were killing me. I knew they were purposely torturing me. They loved to delay gratification, which I hated.

"I want in on that," Tristan said in a gleeful tone.

"We need to plan this and time it perfectly," Sebastian added.

"You fuckers won't get anything if you don't finish what you started," I growled. My hand dropped between my thighs, impatient to take care of the pain they had caused.

"Oh, no you don't." Sebastian stopped me, and Kol pinned my arm above my head.

The fuckers continued to torture me for a few more minutes until I was grunting in frustration.

They found inventive ways to drive me crazy and switched positions to tease me further.

During one of our lovemaking sessions, Kol and I had developed our mental bond. Having three thoughts in my head all at once was overwhelming, so I had learned to close them off when I didn't want their thoughts bombarding mine. However, they demanded that I keep mine open for safety reasons, but I knew they also loved having easy access to my thoughts, especially during sex. I didn't complain because it made them experts on manipulating my body, but I shut them out when needed.

Aside from the bickering, they hadn't given up on competing with each other, especially in bed. The two always tried to keep up with Kol's stamina, so I had been getting very little sleep since reuniting with the princes. However, we had an early class tomorrow, and I stopped after everyone found their release.

"Vi. Don't be like that," Tristan whined.

"You're kidding, right?" Sebastian lay on the bed with his head propped up with a pillow as he stroked his hard length.

Kol sat at the edge and eyed me like a predator. "I'll join you in the shower."

"Oh, no. I know what you're planning. It's not happening, mister," I called over my shoulder.

Kol blurred and pinned me to the wall. "C'mon, Vi. You know once is just prep for me. You wouldn't leave me hanging, would you?"

"It's not fun, is it? Maybe you'll stop doing it to me." I smirked and patted his chest as I tried to push him off.

He stared into my eyes to gauge if I was serious. Then he dropped his head on my shoulder in defeat. After two lungfuls of breath, he said, "Fine. Can I ask for one tiny bite?"

I thought about it for a second, stepped into the bathroom, and gestured for him to follow. He lifted me onto the sink as he exposed his neck to me. I licked his neck and sank my fangs into his flesh as I grabbed his hard steel and started rubbing as I sucked his blood. His hips thrust faster into my hand the harder I sucked, then I felt him sink his fangs into me, and then I felt his hot release into my hand.

He kissed me softly and whispered, "I love you, Vi."

"I love you too, Kol," I said as I recovered from my shaky limbs.

I walked out of the shower and stood in the ridiculous walk-in closet, which held all of our stuff. The apartment had five other bedrooms, which was convenient if we wanted our space.

When I was ready, I found the guys sitting on the sofa in deep discussion. They always stopped when I walked into the room, so I suspected they were keeping something from me.

I eyed them suspiciously, but they acted like nothing was amiss, so I brushed it off. I felt nothing through our bond, so it probably wasn't a big deal.

"Should we go to dinner?" I asked.

"Yeah. I'm looking forward to seeing my friends," Kol said.

"Didn't know you had friends," Sebastian said.

"Shouldn't I be saying that to you since you only hang out with your brother?"

I marched out the door before they gained steam. Sometimes I wished Carlisle were there. He would have kept them in check.

The guys surrounded me, Kol in front, Sebastian behind us, while Tristan held my hand. I wanted to tell them they were paranoid, but then we reached the center of the quad, and a group of students stopped in front of us.

I stepped behind Kol and saw the blond chick whose hand I broke.

"Is it true?" She glared at Kol, and then when she saw me, her eyes turned red. "You whore!" She shrieked and lunged at me. The princes reacted fast, while Kol reached for her neck and slammed her into the ground.

"I will not tolerate any threats to my mate. I don't care who you are; I will end you. Do you hear me?" His voice was icy and slow. He straightened up, and with a menacing gaze, he stared down at the students in front of us. "The Queen is in the dungeons, and the Vampires are at war with the Casters. Those who are against us are fair game. No one messes with my mate. You have been warned." He draped an arm around my shoulder and walked forward without breaking stride.

The crowd parted for him in shock. In contrast, the princes chuckled behind us. My knees shook as fear left my system. I peered at Kol from under my lashes, swooning at the show of badassery. A grin split my lips as I leaned in and whispered, "Remind me to show you how hot that show of manliness was."

His lips twitched, but he said nothing. However, his arms tightened around me.

"Hey, we can be badass too," Tristan grumbled.

"Shut up, idiot," Sebastian said.

"What? Stop being so uptight. You're scaring, Vi."

"It would be best to get the tightwad here. We need a full circle," Seb said.

"Agreed," Kol muttered.

I turned to Tristan in question, but he only swung my backpack on his shoulder to join his own. I wanted to ask them what they meant, but we reached my classroom, and it didn't look like they were leaving, so I looked at the guys in confusion. "Are you all following me in there?"

"Yeah. Haven't you been listening? We're all sticking together," Tristan said as he tugged on my hand and led me to the back of the room.

I opened my mouth to argue, but then I looked around and dropped my gaze, avoiding the stares from the entire room.

My whole body heated from the unwanted attention my men were causing. They had gone overboard. How could they think being attached to my hip twenty-four-seven would help? As much as I loved them, that shit would drive me crazy. Plus, we were drawing unwanted attention.

Mr. Taylor walked in, glanced at us, and said, "It's nice to have the four of you back on campus."

I forced a smile onto my face.

"Okay, class, I know we were in the middle of discussing the effects of how human technology helped suppress the supernaturals, but we will pause on that subject since we have the heirs in this room."

A wave of movement caused me to slink lower into my seat as I tried to avoid the curious glances of the students, along with some hateful glares from the others.

"As you know, the principal aim of this class is to learn from history. It is well known that history often repeats itself. My goal is to teach you and future leaders to learn from our past mistakes so you can do better. We owe it to those innocents who perished needlessly in wars fought over greed and in the name of power." He rummaged through his shelves until he found what he was looking for. He then turned on his projector and set up the slides.

"Let's not pretend war isn't looming between all three races. Just like centuries ago, this was how it all started. However, this time, we are under the watchful eye of humans, whose technology could rival our strength and magic. We also are at a disadvantage since we still don't have the numbers to defeat humans. If anything, our numbers are even more at peril since there are fewer heirs born each year, and without them, the species will perish." He clicked on the slides in succession, showing the carnage of the war. "There is a theory amongst historians about the beginning. It is widely believed that it started with two lovers." He looked around, and his eyes shone with amusement. I followed his gaze, and just like me, everyone had a confused look on their face, including the heirs, so this was something they hadn't heard before.

"Before the Casters ruled over the supernaturals, each royal ruled its race. It was rumored that the Vampire heir and the Caster heir fell in love." Gasps cut through the quiet room. "That's right. As discussed in our previous lesson, other supernaturals lived before Hakuba, the Caster High Priestess, brutally hunted them down. They weren't classified as specific species, so they were believed to be Fae, who we now believe to have returned to their own home, and others who were results of interspecies breeding."

A few of the students chuckled.

"I know it sounds absurd, but it has been proven in the past that it was possible to procreate outside of your species. It was only a few centuries ago that it became impossible. Others believe it's a curse. The same curse that is causing the heirs to dwindle in numbers. However, I digress. The two heirs fell in love, and some scholars believe these two were mates. But their families forced them apart, which made them live bitter and unhappy lives. When it was their turn to rule, they both declined the position, so a power-hungry Caster stepped up and grabbed the opportunity to overpower the sitting Shifter ruler and effectively rule over all supernaturals. The Casters held on to power for decades until the war. We all know how that ended." He paused and looked around the room filled with thick tension. "Did you know that the mate bond is the most sacred bond of nature? It isn't for any supernaturals to mess with. It is believed that to disrupt that bond messes with the balance of nature, and we all know that nature always finds a way to correct itself. If this is true, and this whole thing started with a broken bond between two supernaturals, then I can't help but make a connection to the present. I don't believe in coincidences, so historians like myself wonder why the center of this conflict is mated to several species." He paused, and his gaze settled on me.

Why does he keep calling attention to me?

Relax, babe. Tristan said.

Do you think he's right? Sebastian asked.

Wait until they find out that Carlisle is part of this little band we have. Kol said in amusement.

I groaned. That would call even more attention to me. I struggled not to bang my head on my desk, which the guys picked up on, and I felt their amusement through our bond.

Laugh it up, assholes.

When the bell rang, I was out of my seat and was the first out of the door. The guys struggled to keep up with me as I pushed my way to the locker room. I knew the guys couldn't follow me inside, so I smirked as the door slammed in their faces.

I didn't linger since I felt their growing irritation through our bond, but I glared at them as I met them outside the room, and I didn't say a word since the hall was crowded. We made our way into combat class, which was already half full. As I walked in, two girls wrapped their arms around me and started screaming and jumping.

"I missed you so much, you bitch," Shay said.

"What she said," Lori said as she hooked her arm around mine and led me to the center bleachers.

"I missed you guys too. I was so worried sick. How are you doing?"

"We're good. It's not the same without you," Lori said.

"Tell you more later," Shay whispered as her gaze looked forward. I followed her eyes, and she was staring at Jacob, Logan, and Carla, who other Vampires and Casters surrounded. Were there more students taking this class? That was an awfully large group. Or were they showing solidarity to bully everyone else? They took up the right side of the room with superiority and a glint of malice in their eyes. My eyes narrowed. Did they think they could bully people because they ran in a large group?

Lori stiffened when she noticed what we were looking at. She tucked her hair behind her ears with shaking fingers. I studied her for a moment. She met my eyes, but she shook her head.

I looked at Shay, but she didn't meet my eyes. I surveyed her and noticed a fading bruise on her arm and a scar on her eyebrow.

"Please tell me they did nothing to the two of you," I said in a normal voice, but I kept my gaze on the three Vampires in front. Carla sneered, while Jacob and Logan exchanged knowing glances. Shay grabbed my arm, but I was off my seat before she got a hold of it.

I flashed in front of the Vampires as I thrust my hand to the rest of the room, blocking everyone.

The fuckers in front of me were ready since I felt the attack from the Casters in retaliation. I lifted my lip in a sneer as I pulled on their power. They dropped to the ground in pain. The Casters who didn't attack were left standing with the red-eyed Vampires who bared their fangs at me but didn't make a move.

"Here we are again," I said in a condescending tone. They all glanced at each other, looking for direction on what to do. The wails from the Casters writhing on the floor were distracting, so I gestured to them. "That's right. I've been practicing. Do you know what's happening to them?"

I could hear my mates banging on the barrier I had erected as they tried to reach me through our bond. "I stripped their power. I imagine it's painful being stripped of something that's innately a part of you, especially when it's done so abruptly." I paused as I watched the fear in their eyes, giving them a chance to back off. "Do you know why the evil head priestess wants me? Why she's ready to wage war to get me? It's because I can incapacitate hundreds of you with just a thought." I flicked my hand to the right and blocked the professor, along with Mr.

Wilkins and others standing by the door. I was done playing nice. Let them watch.

"You know, I wanted to live in peace amongst you. I even tolerated your attitude and kept my head bowed. But let me tell you one thing, I will not stand for you hurting my friends. Now, I reckon not all of you were involved, and so far, you haven't attacked me, so I will give you a chance. Leave now and stay neutral for all I care, but this is the only mercy you will get from me." I eyed the remaining Casters and Vampires who stood behind the three.

A few shifted their weight and slowly took a step towards the door, then froze. "It's okay. The barrier will let you through."

Most of them left except for a handful, then Logan tried to flash to the barrier, but he bounced back. I laughed. "What a fucking coward."

Then I turned to the ones who stayed—Vampires and Casters. They stiffened, but their gazes stayed hard on me, and I felt an attack simultaneously from the Casters as the Vampires blurred to get to me. But with a wave of my hand, all of them dropped. "Oh, did I forget to mention? I can pull any magic." I squatted in front of the writhing pieces of shit who were cowardly enough to attack me at the same time. There were probably a dozen or so of them. I wondered how many of them attacked Lori and Shay. The thought made my blood boil. "Let me tell you a little secret. I'm still working on whether I can return the magic I stole." I chuckled.

Logan's nose bled, but he was on his feet, looking murderous. He didn't make a move, though. I made sure to save the assholes for last. "So have at it, you three. What will it be?

There's only one of me and still three of you." I made a *get me* gesture. "How many of you were there when you attacked my friends?" My eyes narrowed. "No answer? Are you only brave with numbers behind you, or do you only attack when our backs are turned?"

"It's not fair since you can strip us of our powers," Jacob said, his voice cracking at the end. He was brave, and I'd give him that.

"Fair enough. After all, this is a combat class, so how about I promise not to use my other abilities, except my Vampire ones, as we fight it out. In return, you leave my friends alone. If you break that promise, I will hunt you and your families and strip your entire line of power."

I flinched as my three mates almost broke through our bond. They didn't like my proposal, and I didn't dare glance their way. I had a feeling I would lose my nerve if I did. I also had a feeling that Mr. Wilson and my friends weren't happy with me right then. It probably wasn't wise to give the Casters any information, or they would find ways to subdue me. Oh, well. They knew about mimic and siphon, so it wasn't like it was a secret.

"How do we know you wouldn't cheat?" Carla asked.

I shrugged. "You don't. It's the only shot you got. Otherwise, I snap my fingers, and you join them." I gestured to the ones on the floor. Some were sobbing silently, and the others were rocking side to side. I tried not to feel too bad about it. Some aimed to kill and deliver death attacks, so they deserved it.

"Last chance." I tapped my foot impatiently.

The three glanced at each other, and some understanding must have been exchanged since they all straightened their shoulders, and Carla tipped up her chin. I waved my hand once again, and we were at the center, enclosed in a barrier no one could cross and the ones in the room were now free.

I briefly saw the professors going to the ones on the floor.

The three Vampires wiped their looks of surprise from being moved without their permission, but they recovered quickly. With no preamble, all three blurred and attacked me at once. I knew they were cowards. However, I moved faster and punched one in the face while I wrapped my arm around Carla's neck and spun us around, then kicked one in the gut. As soon as both guys were down, I twisted Carla's neck and dropped her to the ground. I stopped right before I heard her neck snap, but I was sure she was out cold.

I waited for the other two to recover since, unlike them, I didn't fight dirty. Just like before, they attacked simultaneously. I leaped in the air and grabbed onto Logan's face while wrapping my legs around Jacob's neck and twisted my body. I took Logan with us as we dropped to the floor. Again, I strained my muscles and controlled our drop to ensure I didn't snap their necks. I stood up and waved my hand to dissipate the barrier.

My three mates, along with my two best friends, rushed at me, but I held out a hand and said, "Stop."

Surprisingly, they all listened, while everyone else stayed still, eyeing me in trepidation.

"I don't want to hear it. I'm still feeling murderous, so I suggest you take care of them before I finish the job. We can talk about it later." I paused long enough to make sure they heard me then marched out the door.

Mr. Taylor and Mr. Wilson stepped away and gave me room to walk out. I heard footsteps behind me and saw Tristan following. I took a deep breath and let it out slowly, and slowed down enough for him to catch up. He walked next to me, but for once, he was quiet and didn't touch me.

As the adrenalin seeped out of my veins, guilt settled into my stomach. I probably took things too far, but they crossed the line by touching my friends. I blinked away tears of frustration and made my way back to the room without a word.

Chapter 9

Kol

MR. WILSON CLEARED the room, leaving Sebastian, Mr. Taylor, the injured, Shay, and Lori. "Gary, could you please escort the girls to their dorm and make sure they get there safely? We wouldn't want another incident if something were to happen to Vi's friends." Mr. Wilson addressed Mr. Taylor as he rubbed the bridge of his nose.

"Certainly." He gestured to Shay and Lori, who followed him silently out of the room.

"What are we going to do with them?" Sebastian indicated to the Casters and Vampires on the floor.

"I will have them taken to the infirmary for now and meet with the Kings before I proceed."

"I want the Vampires in my custody."

He nodded absently.

"I already have people on their way to pick them up. They will be dealt with accordingly."

He paused and looked at me. "What will happen to them?"

"They broke the King's order. Father made it clear not to take sides in the war. They broke Vampire rules."

"Very well."

We waited with tension as they moved the injured out of the room. As soon as it was empty, Mr. Wilson slumped in a bleacher. "We need to talk, but it isn't safe here. Let's go to my office."

We'd quickly found that being mated to Vi meant that the three of us were connected as well. We were able to communicate telepathically without Vi. We had been conferring with Tristan, and he had been keeping us updated on Vi's status. He said that she'd been holding back tears and wasn't talking much. I was sure the guilt would get to her soon, so we needed to be there to comfort her.

I let out a frustrated sigh as I recalled how the attack on her felt. It was like someone had jammed a stake in my chest every time they hit her with a killing blow.

We were immobilized and useless. It was eye-opening, something we needed to discuss since we needed to do better in protecting our mate in times of danger. I hated to admit that the barrier had been something of a blessing since it allowed me to see and realize that Vi could take care of herself. Otherwise, I would have ripped apart everyone in the room. However, I would still prefer it if she stopped doing it.

Mr. Wilson waved his hand to seal the room and sat down heavily on the sofa. "What a fucking mess." He massaged the bridge of his nose. "What happened?"

We shook our heads.

"I mean, I got the gist of what happened with her speech, but..."

"How did you know to come?" Sebastian interrupted.

"We all felt it. I don't know how to describe it, but a strong feeling of fear had me rushing out of my office. It's stupid to go close to something you fear, but I drew us to it. It was a massive power, and we felt her anger. I surmised that the ones behind the barrier were protected since the fear faded once she erected the barrier around us as well." He shuddered as he glanced to the side with a faraway look. Then, after a moment, he looked at us with reluctance. "I hate to bring this up, but I'm convinced, now more than ever, that the Casters can't get their hands on someone like her. Please don't get mad at me for saying this, but someone with that much power is too dangerous."

"What are you implying?" Sebastian asked while I straightened up. As much as I liked the dean and saw him almost like an uncle, I would destroy him if he suggested harming Vi.

"I'm not implying anything. I'm simply warning you. With great power comes great responsibility and great danger. There's a reason her power is unnatural. She has the power to enslave thousands of people and destroy the world. Please don't be defensive. I'm simply voicing out a warning."

"For what purpose?" I asked to make sure I understood where he was coming from. We couldn't fight too many enemies.

"As her mates, it is your responsibility to make sure she doesn't abuse her power. Someone like her couldn't afford to make mistakes or lose her temper. A dark deed takes a toll on your soul, and once you cross that line, there is no going back. She has a good soul right now. I know that. I've read her energy, but what if she had crossed that line tonight? What if she had killed everyone? Something that heinous taints the soul. Decades from now, she might turn into a very powerful monster. Someone that has the potential to enslave us all."

No one spoke—not even Tristan, who we'd allowed to hear what the dean had to say. I felt our shared anger quickly ripped out of us as Mr. Wilson explained his fear.

Fuck, Sebastian said.

Why did he have to put that in our heads? Tristan complained.

We'll need to make sure that won't happen. We need to keep her safe, even from herself.

Agreed, Tristan said.

We really need the fucking Caster here with us. We can't do this ourselves. Sebastian threw me a pointed look from the other sofa.

The sooner, the better, Tristan said.

One problem at a time, I replied to my bond mates. Out loud, I said, "As her mates, we will make sure she never crosses that line."

"I beg your pardon, Kol. But she disabled everyone with a wave of her hand. Including you, the heirs—her mates. How do you plan on doing that?" Mr. Wilson asked.

"I admit we have our work cut out for us." Sebastian pushed off the seat, crossed his arms, and stood in an agitated manner. "There are too many things going on. We're fighting the Casters, the students, and now we need to worry about Vi's power."

I'd never seen Sebastian so flustered in the past. He and his brother always took things in their stride, but I guess he was just good at keeping it all in. I felt a pang of camaraderie towards him as he shared his frustration. Although I felt my bond with them, I didn't honestly know what it meant. That was why we still bickered like old times. However, as we put our guards down and trusted each other, this proved we were in this together. We just needed Carlisle to complete our bond.

I think this was why Vi required all the heirs as her mate. She was too strong, and she needed all of us by her side to support her. We needed to get Carlisle sooner rather than later.

Sebastian turned to me and studied me for a moment, then nodded.

Yeah, I think you're right, Tristan agreed. We hadn't tested the range of our bond, but it would come in handy in keeping Vi safe.

"You are not alone. You have good people around you," Mr. Wilson said.

"We appreciate your wisdom and your help," I replied. "We will need to get Carlisle soon. Any input will be helpful."

"Why do you need Carlisle?" He raised a brow.

Sebastian nodded.

I guess you can tell him. It's not like we have a choice, Tristan said.

"We believe he is Vi's fourth mate. We need him," I answered.

He stared at me for a moment, then nodded. "That makes so much sense. I've always wondered why the four of you had taken so much interest in Viola. Gary had already voiced out his theory. It makes me feel better that a Caster is part of her mates. I believe you are right. I can see how his presence could help."

The room had gone quiet. "I will make some phone calls. Once I know more, I'll reach out to you, and we can formulate a plan. I understand this needs to happen soon." He got up.

"Thank you." I followed him to the door.

"Thank you, Mr. Wilson," Sebastian said over his shoulder.

Sebastian and I didn't rush back to our room since Tristan had reported that Vi was in the bathroom, still not speaking to him.

Tristan, do you think you can watch Vi a little longer? Sebastian asked, and I flashed him a confused look.

Sure.

Thanks, bro. Kol and I will need to speak to the Kings before this gets out of hand.

I nodded in agreement. "I will call a meeting."

I led Sebastian to my car, and we drove to the city. We received confirmation to meet the Kings at the Shifter's tower.

When we got there, father and Rahl were having a drink in the living room.

My father gave me a hug, which was something I was still getting used to. He had been acting more like himself since the incident with Delia. Perhaps he found closure on my mother's death, or perhaps Vi reminded him of the time they were all happy. He had been invested in protecting Vi, and maybe it gave him purpose and a reason to live again.

"Tell us what happened." Rahl looked serious.

"We figured it was better that this comes from us..." Sebastian eyed the Kings and gestured for me to continue.

I told them everything, including the discussion we had with Mr. Wilson.

Tell them about Carlisle, Tristan added.

The Kings smiled with the revelation that Carlisle was mated to Vi. "I knew she was special when I took her in. I just didn't know how crucial she is in our future," Rahl mused.

"If I had met her sooner, I would have known who she was," Father answered.

"What are we missing?" Sebastian said in an irritated tone.

"We had speculated that Viola would be an instrument in breaking the curse on the supernaturals." Rahl set his drink down.

"Yes. She will lead our people to a new beginning," Father added cryptically.

What the hell are they talking about? Tristan voiced my confusion. I glanced at Sebastian, who shrugged, clearly lost as I was.

"What aren't you telling us?" I asked carefully.

Father crossed his leg and stared at Sebastian and me intently. "Our people are at the brink of extinction. The Casters killed off any beings that could challenge their power. We believe Vi can unite our people and make sure that the Casters wouldn't wage war amongst the supernaturals again."

"Yes. That's why it's imperative for Vi to learn her powers and to make sure that the Casters can't get their hands on her." Rahl leaned over his knee.

"We will make it a priority to extricate Carlisle from the Casters." Father glanced at Rahl, who nodded in agreement.

"One or two of you will need to head the mission. Vi can't be anywhere near the Casters' territory, so make sure she stays on campus." Rahl said.

"Let us know as soon as possible. In the meantime, we need to get back to our mate." Sebastian stood.

"We will take care of the fallout from the families who were stripped of their powers." Rahl thumped Sebastian's back.

"I will take care of the Vampires who disobeyed my orders. My people will need to learn that their King does not tolerate insubordination. I have been lenient for a long time, but that stops now."

I nodded at him with pride. It was nice to see my father back instead of the empty shell he had become.

We came back to Tristan holding Vi as she slept. We crawled into bed with them, which released the tension I had felt all day.

We need to make sure she doesn't get put in that situation again.

Yeah. We need to protect her soul, Tristan said.

First, we need to guide her in dealing with what happened tonight. She needs to see that violence is not always the answer.

Sebastian's statement amused Tristan.

What I meant was, her violence is not the answer. She should leave it to her mates, Sebastian said.

I agree. She can't keep sidelining us. She needs to know that her actions have significant consequences, I added.

We were quiet for a while, but I sensed that my bond mates were still awake, possibly too many thoughts swirling in my brain.

Do you think the Kings were referring to the curse Mr. Taylor talked about in class?

Sebastian and Tristan took a moment to respond. *Do we really believe in the curse?* Tristan asked.

It must be true if both kings agree, Sebastian said.

Should we tell Vi? I asked in hesitation since I didn't want to add any more pressure on her yet.

The others must have thought the same thing because Sebastian said, *Only as a last resort.*

Yeah, only if we couldn't get her to see reason, Tristan followed.

Vi had her arm around Tristan with their legs intertwined. I moved closer, so her back was touching my chest, and I placed my hand on her hip. I saw Sebastian hold her hand over Tristan's side, and one by one, we drifted off to sleep.

Chapter 10

Vi

I FELT MY MATES CRAWL into bed with me, but I kept my eyes shut and my thoughts inaccessible to them.

I was a monster, and I didn't deserve their love. My temper got to me, and I abused the power I had over those who were weak. It wasn't a lie when I said I didn't know if I could give back the powers I took.

Now I understood why my kind was hunted into extinction. We were dangerous, and we evoked fear in everyone. Even though I didn't consider myself evil, I couldn't assuredly say I wouldn't repeat my actions when angered. I could become a tyrant as long as I had those powers and no-one to rival mine. I wouldn't differ from Lucille Pruitt, the evil head priestess.

I didn't dare move until I heard all three of them get into deep, rhythmic breathing. I stayed awake all night, racking my brains for how I could tamp down my powers. It wasn't worth it. I was being hunted, and now I was a danger to everyone. If I could have given them back and gone back to being a regular human, I would have.

I might have dozed off for a few hours, but my eyes opened as soon as I felt my mates stir.

"Hey, are you okay?" Sebastian asked as he leaned on his elbow and brushed the hair off my face.

I took a deep breath but didn't respond. Tristan pulled me closer to his body and placed a gentle kiss on my shoulder while Kol grabbed my hand. I could feel their concern through our bond as they tried to gain access to my thoughts.

The guilt filled my chest once again with the addition of pushing them away. I could feel their frustration and worry through our bond, but I wasn't ready to open up. They watched me intently, and I knew I should say something, but no words came to mind. I just wanted to be left alone.

However, I owed it to them to try, so I said, "I will be. I'm sorry. I don't mean to shut you guys out, but I just need time for myself. Is that okay?" I kept my gaze on the ceiling and didn't meet their eyes. I just wished to close my eyes and make everything disappear, but I knew in doing so, I'd be pushing them away. I needed them, even if I wasn't ready to open up just yet.

God, I was selfish. I wanted them to leave me alone, but I also didn't want them to go. My eyes burned with unshed tears, so I shut my eyes.

I felt the three of them press a gentle kiss on my skin, and Kol said, "We're right here when you're ready to talk." He then released my hand and got up. The other two followed, and once I heard the click of the door, I let the tears flow.

I didn't move from my spot except to go to the bathroom. I was in and out of sleep until Sebastian brought in a tray of food.

"Vi. I got you a bit of everything since I wasn't sure what you wanted to eat."

I flashed him a weak smile as a thank you.

"Nope. You are getting up and eating something. I won't force you to leave the bed, but I'm not leaving until you eat." I now knew why he was the one with the food tray. Tristan was the playful one, and Kol was the quiet, intense one. However, Seb was the one who didn't have a problem telling the brutal truth. Carlisle was the responsible leader.

I frowned at the thought since he wasn't my mate, but I had always thought of him as part of the group. He said Casters didn't have mates, but they had someone compatible with their magic. The last time I saw him, he said we would talk about our magic, but that was before everything went to hell. I wondered how he was doing. I hoped he was safe from the evil bitch's clutches, or I would rain down hell on her coven.

I got up abruptly as fear and guilt filled me. The simmering fury was always just beyond the surface, and I was quick to anger. It was something I couldn't control, but I vowed to myself to never use my power in rage again. It would be best if I didn't use my abilities at all.

"What's wrong?" Sebastian reached to cup my cheek.

I allowed myself to lean into his touch for a second, and the sudden anger within me subsided. "I was just wondering how Carlisle is doing. Do you think he's okay?"

His eyes flared briefly, and my stomach sank. Great, I had been pushing them away, and my first words to him were about another man—who wasn't my mate. "I just wanted to be sure he was safe, that's all," I said in a small voice, then reached for the fruit bowl as my way of making amends.

After a couple of bites, I set the bowl down.

Sebastian raised a brow and pointedly looked at the discarded bowl.

I kissed his cheek and said, "Thank you for taking care of me. I really don't deserve you three."

His eyes narrowed in response, but I was already turning away and lying back down. I felt his eyes on me for a few minutes before I heard a sigh and the tinkling of the tray as he walked out of the room.

Although my thoughts continued to swirl with guilt and anger, I slept for most of the afternoon. I vaguely felt my mates check in on me, but I continued to ignore them.

"Vi, wake up." Kol shook my shoulder gently.

I opened my eyes, and for a moment, I was happy to see him. Then the memory and guilt of what I had done flooded me, and I turned my back on Kol instead.

With a heavy sigh, I felt Kol shift closer, and then he pulled me to his chest. I felt the darkness inside me subside as he touched me, and I allowed myself to sink into his embrace.

"What am I gonna do with you?" he whispered into my neck. I had the urge to tilt my neck so he could get better access, but the feeling was fleeting.

"Do I need to tie you up and fuck this nasty feeling off you?" he murmured as he traced his nose on my shoulder.

My mouth twitched, but I stayed quiet.

"Tell me what you need, Vi." He slid his hand under my sleep shirt, and he splayed his large hand on my stomach. His fingers drew lazy circles on my side, which had me looking up at him with desire. His touch kept the guilt and darkness at bay, and I didn't want him to stop. I wanted him to erase the feeling inside of me, so I reached for his face and kissed him with desperation.

He didn't waste time and was on top of me the next moment.

I heard my shirt rip, followed by my panties. Before I could protest, he pressed his mouth on mine. Usually, Kol liked to take his time, but not that day. He was inside me instantly, and his fangs descended on my skin. His bite always brought me over the edge, and I knew he wanted the same, so I bit his shoulder as I shuddered a release.

Without having time to recover, I was being shifted off the bed, and I opened my eyes to find Tristan in front of me. I sank onto his shaft and felt Sebastian step behind me. I didn't even see them come in. My time with Kol was quick, but I knew he was just getting started.

I moaned from the feeling of both my heirs inside me, but I wanted more. I needed to erase the darkness inside me, and I needed to forget.

"More," I said as I reached for Kol, who obeyed and caressed his lips to mine. However, I didn't want gentle, so I tilted his neck and bit into his flesh hard. He grunted and placed my hand in between his thighs. I moaned loudly, and my breathing had become erratic while Sebastian and Tristan slammed into my body with a punishing pace. I pulled my head away from Kol and leaned on Sebastian's chest. I felt Kol's lips on my neck. Goosebumps crawled up my spine in anticipation of Kol's fangs sinking into my skin. I gripped down as I felt Kol suck my blood into his mouth, while Tristan and Sebastian grunted their hot releases inside of me. The three of us collapsed onto the bed as I kept my face buried in Tristan's chest, while Sebastian's legs tangled with mine. I reached over and draped my arm over Kol, who was next to Tristan.

"How are you feeling, Vi?" Kol asked.

My hand paused from tracing his skin, and I felt Tristan and Sebastian stiffen. I shrugged and said, "That helped. You three drive the darkness away."

"If you want to continue, I am at your service. I've been dying to tie you to the bed." Kol smirked.

I laughed, which made me feel lighter inside. His eyes darkened, and I knew he would carry on with his promise.

I WAS READY TO GO BACK to class the next day, even if my mates and I had only had a few hours of sleep. I thoroughly enjoyed their games in the bedroom. Not that I would ever admit that out loud, but I wouldn't mind if they did that again.

A smile made its way to my lips as I got dressed. I was ready to face the consequences of my actions. No more feeling sorry for myself.

Shay and Lori threw their arms around me while I was stacking food onto my tray. I returned their hugs, careful not to spill my food.

"We've been so worried about you," Shay said, grabbing a plate of everything, and Lori followed. Those two always had an abundant appetite.

"I know, I'm sorry. I just needed to process." I shrugged and followed the two to our usual table.

"Seriously, how are you?" Lori asked.

I wanted to shrug and brush off their concern, but I learned from my mates' persistence that shutting everyone out allowed the dark thoughts to fester.

I also remembered my mates' warning. With great powers comes great responsibility, and I needed everyone's support to keep my powers under control. So, I glanced at the two from under my lashes and said, "I'm coping. It might take time, but I'll get there." I smiled and grabbed their hands across the table. "Especially if I have my friends by my side."

"Damn straight. And don't you forget it." Shay held my eyes until I nodded. She smiled, and the tension lining her cute features eased as she took a large bite of her pizza.

However, Lori didn't let go of my hand. "We wanted to see you yesterday, but your mates were ultra-protective."

"Yeah, they were surlier than usual. We could only get a growl out of them and maybe one-word answers," Shay said between bites.

"We wanted to say thank you for what you did and that...." Uncertainty crossed Lori's face, but she straightened and continued, "we wanted to say we don't think any less of you," she said in a rush and flashed me an apologetic look.

"Of course not. It's what we expect from our Alpha. You should hear what the Shifters are saying about you." Shay didn't look up from her food as I stared at her in shock.

I glanced at Lori, and she nodded. "Yes. It's true."

"You mean I didn't scare them off?" I asked with my brows raised.

"Oh, no. Of course they're terrified of you." Shay waved a spoon in my direction.

I frowned at her, but Shay only had her eyes on her food.

Lori jumped in and said, "Fear comes naturally to Shifters. It's normal to fear our Alpha. But we also want to feel assured our Alpha is strong enough to defend the pack. You proved that yesterday. You were protecting us and unleashed your badass to those who wished us harm."

I thought about what she said.

"Since the war started, the Shifters have been divided. Although we love and respect our King, some feared he would take the political route at the expense of our safety. Families had gone underground in fear. Don't get me wrong, we understand the King's actions. He has to think of the greater good and consider the best course for the future. But it didn't take away the feeling of lack of safety at the moment," Lori continued.

Shay toyed with her food. "With your actions, you showed you place the safety of the pack first." She took a bite of a cookie. "Yep. You, my friend, are a badass. It's a good feeling to have you on our side."

I hardly touched my eggs, and I glanced at my mates at the other table. For the first time since the incident, I opened my thoughts to them and felt their anxiety ease.

Hey, babe. Please don't shut me out again, Tristan said.

Yeah, it's like something is missing when you shut us out, Sebastian added.

It's true what your friends said. Even some Vampires feel the same. I know once Carlisle joins our group, the Casters will feel confident in your protection. Kol met my eyes from across the table.

Speechless, I gaped at my mates. How could they be okay with what I'd done? It was still wrong.

I know it is, but sometimes in a war, you must do what's needed, even if it isn't pretty, Sebastian said.

Don't worry; we will be by your side to ensure you don't abuse your powers. Tristan grinned.

I smiled and met my mates' eyes, grateful I had them in my life.

"We need to go, or we're going to be late." Shay jumped up from her seat and tugged on Lori's arm.

"We'll meet up with you for lunch," Lori said.

"Yeah, later," Shay said from over her shoulder.

I chuckled as I watched them.

"Are you ready?" Sebastian asked.

"Yeah."

"We're skipping Professor Wilkins' class today and meeting up with the dean." Tristan grabbed my book bag from the floor.

"Am I in trouble?"

"No. We just need to discuss some things." Kol grabbed my other hand and led us out of the cafeteria.

"So when are we going to rescue Carlisle?" I was done pretending that he wasn't important to me. The other three seemed to accept him as part of our group already, so it was time for me to acknowledge that he could be my potential fourth mate. If he wanted to be. He didn't seem to like the idea that our magic was linked.

Kol kissed the side of my head. "Don't worry. And he is drawn to you just as much as we were." I must have broadcasted my thoughts and feelings through our bond.

"Yep, there is no way he wouldn't want the bond." Tristan looked back and smirked.

"Yeah, it's like not wanting a limb or something. You are a part of us, Vi. never doubt that." Sebastian glanced at me with a firm expression on his face.

Warmth filled my chest, and I pushed my intense feeling through our bonds since words were inadequate in expressing how much they meant to me.

So, should we plan to rescue him soon? Please.

"That's one thing we're discussing." Kol lips lifted before he knocked on the dean's door.

"Way ahead of you," Tristan said as he walked in.

I frowned and followed them to the couch by the fireplace.

"Glad you could make it, Viola," Dean Wilson said.

"Am I in trouble? How is everyone doing? The ones who..." My hands twisted in my lap, unable to finish my statement.

"No, you're not in trouble. The ones who were stripped of powers are doing fine. I mean, as fine as they could be given that they're now powerless."

"I can try to give them their powers back," I offered.

"I had a long meeting with the Kings, and they concluded that, given their actions, they are now sufficiently punished. King Henry was going to execute them but kept them as is after some further discussions. Of course, he met with their parents and told them his decision."

I glanced at Kol, who nodded in confirmation.

"King Rahl did the same, but he would have imprisoned them otherwise."

"What about the Casters?"

"We are at war, and they chose the wrong side. We believe that, eventually, they will come to be grateful they still live amongst us."

It seemed wrong. I wasn't comfortable with their decisions. Not that I didn't think they deserved it, but that I was getting out of my horrible actions unscathed.

"Don't look too upset, Viola. I will be the first to admit that I was concerned with your actions. I would be lying if I didn't say that it makes me wary of the future. However, I believe that with the right support and guidance, you won't abuse your powers."

I glanced at my mates as desperation filled me. They must have felt my feelings since they all reached out to touch me. "What happens if I lose control?" I asked in a small voice.

"You won't," Sebastian said.

"We won't let you." Tristan squeezed my hand.

"Trust us and trust yourself, Vi," Kol said behind me.

I nodded, even though I still felt slightly uneasy. However, there wasn't anything I could do except to try my darndest not to fuck up. The dean must have seen the determination in my face because he gave me a nod of approval and flashed me a smile.

"Another reason we are here is to discuss Carlisle's extraction from the Casters' domain."

My heart leaped in both joy at seeing Carlisle and in fear. What if something happened to him? No matter what, we would rescue him. I didn't care who I had to face.

"...it is why it needs to be a small group." Mr. Wilson said.

"What? What did I miss?" I sat up straight.

"Vi. You can't go. It has to be Kol and me," Sebastian said.

"Why am I always left behind?" Tristan complained.

"Yes, why are we left behind? We're a unit, and we should stick together." I crossed my arms.

"Didn't you hear what Mr. Wilson said?" Kol asked.

I just glared at him in response, not wanting to admit that I wasn't listening.

"Tris, we talked about this. You know one of us needs to stay with Vi." Sebastian turned to Tristan.

"Yeah, but I never agreed. Maybe you should stay behind. I'm just as capable," he insisted stubbornly.

"I don't care who goes with me." Kol shrugged.

"Maybe you should stay, and we both go." Tristan gestured to Sebastian.

Kol shrugged like he didn't care either way, but then Sebastian added, "We need his skills, and he knows the area."

"Then it's settled. I'm going." Tristan leaned back in his chair with a stubborn jut of his chin.

"Fine," Sebastian growled.

"What about me?" I asked.

"NO." The three of them responded at the same time.

My face burned in anger and worry, so I tuned them out as they planned the extraction without me. Their planning didn't last long; it sounded like they had been planning this for a while, so they just needed to make sure they got new intel from the dean to make certain adjustments to their plans.

My attempts to convince them to let me go didn't result in anything. They'd been adamant that I stayed far away from the Casters' territory.

We skipped classes for the rest of the day since they planned on leaving that night, which was fine because I was still stewing in anger when we reached our rooms.

"Don't be mad. You know we need to keep you away from the Casters." Tristan pulled me close and peered into my eyes.

I refused to look at him since I disagreed with the plan.

Kol stepped in behind me and kissed my neck. "Taking you would change the mission. Every Caster we encountered would want to apprehend you, and we would need to take more men with us."

"They're right. The best plan is to go in and out on a stealth mission, attracting no trouble," Sebastian said.

Their plan was sound, but it didn't ease my worry.

"C'mon, babe. You know I can't go on a mission with a clear mind if I know I've upset you." Tristan used his alluring voice.

I narrowed my eyes and stopped the smile that threatened to show on my lips. He knew I was weak for my mates and quickly gave in to their demands.

"I'll be worried the whole time you two are gone."

"Keep your mind open, and we will maintain communication with you at all times." Kol pulled me tighter into his chest.

"Isn't that dangerous?" I asked.

"We will only communicate if it's necessary. We'll make sure we allow you to read our minds so you know we're okay," Tristan added.

"You guys have thought of everything."

"We've been practicing for several days. We didn't want to be cut off from each other like last time. That was pure hell," Sebastian said from the sofa.

"Okay, but promise me you two will be careful."

"We promise. If everything goes well, we should be back tonight or tomorrow," Kol said.

"Okay. What time do you leave?"

"We just need to wait for nightfall, and then we can go," Tristan answered.

"We should make sure we spend our time wisely." Kol's fangs scraped my skin, which had me arching in his direction.

I could feel his smile as he continued to tease me.

"You three enjoy. I'll make sure everything is in order before you leave," Sebastian said, which we barely heard since we were lost in each other.

We spent several rounds together until we fell asleep. They got up from bed when Sebastian entered the room and told them it was time.

I didn't follow them since I was certain I would start panicking again. They both pressed their lips on mine and said their goodbyes, and then they were out of the door. Sebastian joined me shortly after and held me. I made sure I could read their thoughts and didn't relax until I was convinced I could still tap into their heads, regardless of the distance.

I sent them feelings of awe for their bravery and love for risking their lives to get Carlisle for me.

After a couple of hours of me lying still with my eyes closed as I focused on Kol and Tristan, Sebastian pinned my arms over my head and said, "Stop obsessing. You need a distraction."

I shook my head to say no. Now wasn't the time, but he didn't take no for an answer. It only took a few moments of his mouth on my skin to give in to his demands. He kept me distracted, especially when I woke up from a light sleep and realized Kol and Tristan hadn't returned. Before panic set in, Sebastian took it upon himself to make sure I was thoroughly distracted. I lost track of time, but I was so exhausted from Sebastian's ministrations on my body that I finally fell asleep.

Chapter 11

Tristan

MR. WILSON'S INTEL was on point. We made it inside the Casters' domain without detection. From there, it was easy to find the compound of the Solaris Coven, and it had the largest mansion seen from the entrance.

I grew up in the towers with Rahl. Since my parents found out that my brother and I were heirs, they moved us into the safety of the towers. My parents couldn't handle the pressure, so they had moved out and visited now and then, but Rahl was the one who raised us.

My mother adopted Sebastian when he was a baby. His parents were killed in an attack when he was only a few weeks old. Rahl couldn't take him, so my mom took him in, and we had been brothers ever since. My mom hated growing up in a family of the heir, and she turned her back on that life when their sister died—it was just the three siblings, so Seb and I were still blood, even though we weren't technically full brothers, however, in everything that counts, he is my brother.

She hoped her children wouldn't have to deal with the burden, but to her disappointment, they recognized both of us as Alphas before we were even a year old. Sometimes I wondered what it would be like if we grew up in a community like this instead of the towers.

Kol snorted, having heard my thoughts. "I'm certain Carlisle is wondering how it would be to grow up in the tower since that future was his right and was ripped away from him by the evil wench." he said in a low voice. We didn't dare use our bond to communicate since we didn't know the Casters' security around the area. They could trace all kinds of magic, so we didn't take any risks. We spoke in low volumes since Casters didn't have sharp senses.

We leaped over the tall walls on the east side and made sure we stayed in the shadows as we made our way to Carlisle's window. Mr. Wilson said his room had a corner window on the east side. "There are several windows. Which one is his?"

"I'm guessing it's the largest one."

"Not the time to guess," I hissed.

"Do you have a better idea?" Kol snapped.

I stared at the several windows above us and shrugged. "No. Let's go with your suggestion." I eyed the distance between the crawling vines on the side of the structure, then leaped and latched on to the thick vines. I looked up and saw a shadow streak up the wall and muttered, "Show off." Kol was like a freaking spider. He scaled the wall quickly, which I needed to do since I sensed the vines disconnecting from the wall.

I heard the window creek and saw Kol pulling himself up on the windowsill. "He stuck his head out after a few minutes and whispered, "All clear."

I joined him inside the dark room as my eyes adjusted. It looked like we had the right room since it was clean, with male decor. It was a large room with a sleigh bed, leather seats, and mahogany furniture.

We heard someone walk down the hall, and Kol and I ducked into the door. We were in the bathroom. Good thing Kol left the door cracked so we could see who walked in.

It took my eyesight a moment to adjust to the sudden bright light, but there was no mistaking Carlisle as he shut the door and walked towards the open window.

He stopped a few feet away, and his shoulders tensed. "Whoever you are, show yourself now."

Kol stepped out of the room with his hands up. "Hey, take it easy. It's just us."

A look of surprise morphed into confusion as his eyes bounced between Kol and me. After a moment, his shoulders relaxed, and he crossed his arms. "What's going on? Why are you two here? Is Vi..."

"She's okay." I cut him off before he said her name. We wanted to be extra careful in case he was being bugged.

"We need you to come back to the academy with us," Kol said.

Carlisle's brows drew together, and I held my hands up. "Is this room secured?"

His eyes grew, and after a moment, he waved his arms, and I felt energy escape him. "It is now."

"What's going on?"

"We're here to take you back to the academy." I looked out the window and shut the heavy drapes. "Get packing, magic boy."

Kol shook his head.

My lips quivered a bit to ease Carlisle into the idea of going with us. "We all know that you're Vi's mate. She needs you."

Carlisle straightened up and crossed his arms. He was still in denial over their bond. "I thought you said she was okay."

"It's a long story, and we can't get into the details right now. I would like to get out of Casters' territory and back to my mate before sunrise," Kol said in a curt tone.

Carlisle raised a brow and squared his shoulders, clearly not impressed with Kol's attitude. I didn't even want to think about how our dynamics would work with the four of us together. However, aside from some snide comments, overall, I would say we got along reasonably well. We worked great when it came to Vi's safety. I couldn't see why it would be different with Carlisle.

"I can't go. I'm needed here," he said firmly.

"What is more important than protecting your mate? This war is about her; if you want to make a difference, you need to be by her side. She needs you," Kol said with a glare.

Carlisle was quiet for a moment, then his shoulders sagged. "C'mon, we need to speak with my aunt." He walked towards the door then paused as he noticed we weren't following. "Don't worry. You're safe inside the mansion. No other Casters can come in unless we allow them to. My grandmother's security was still intact from when she was the head priestess. As long as the coven lives here, the walls will not be breached."

I felt the tension drain from Kol, which reflected mine. We'd been on high alert since leaving campus. The kings sent several of their trusted men, who were scattered around the territory. Amelia's team was going to meet us there once we were ready to go.

We had gone into radio silence since stepping foot inside the Casters' territory as an extra precaution. We were only to use our comms in an emergency.

Carlisle led us past several rooms and two flights of stairs, where Casters and some children could be heard from another room. Carlisle pressed his finger to his lips as a sign for us to be quiet when we reached the bottom of the stairs.

I shared a confused look with Kol. *I thought we were safe here.*

Yeah, I don't like it, Tristan responded through our bond. Like me, he probably assumed it would be safe to communicate under the protection of the Parkers. I didn't chance contacting Vi because I didn't know how the distance worked. It might have been something others could detect.

Kol paused and glared at Carlisle, who shook his head and chuckled. "I don't want everyone making a big fuss. My family is crazy," he whispered.

He led us down the hall, our footsteps light against the marble floor. We heard arguing from children and teens, their voices carrying over the noise of the television.

We made it to a large kitchen with stainless steel appliances and a giant island.

How many people live here? Kol asked.

I shrugged and followed Carlisle to the stove with several pots with steam billowing from them. From the smell of it, the pots didn't contain dinner.

A lady, probably the age of my father, stood over the pots. She had short hair with some grey undertones. She looked up as Carlisle approached, but then her hand paused stirring when she spotted us, and then her eyes flicked to Carlisle.

The lady had an uncanny resemblance to Rose, the evil priestess' second in command. The same lady that betrayed her coven and helped with the downfall of Margaret—the former head priestess and Carlisle's grandmother.

Kol and I exchanged another uneasy look, but we didn't show any fear. Although we trusted Carlisle with our safety, we didn't trust any of the Casters. As proven, they were prone to betrayal.

The lady untied her apron from the back and set it aside on top of the counter. She gestured for us to have a seat on the stools by the island. We walked to it but didn't sit down.

She settled herself on the chair and turned to Carlisle, who sat to her right. "What's going on?" Her eyes narrowed at us suspiciously.

"They are Viola's mates." He did a double-take as he glanced at me and said, "Wait, Kol, when did...."

I waved him off and grunted, "That's not important right now." He must have been able to sense our bond with Vi.

He studied me for a moment, then turned to the lady. "Kol, Tristan, this is my Aunt Adelle, the head of the Solaris coven." He turned to the lady and continued before anyone could say anything. "They are here to take me back to the academy. They said Vi needs me."

The lady appraised Carlisle, and then her gaze turned to Tristan and me. She stayed quiet for a few moments, then she said, "I told you before you need to be with Viola. Stop denying your bond." Her eyes remained soft and shone with love and kindness, so unlike her sister's.

Carlisle opened his mouth, but another lady who looked more like Carlisle walked in. "What's going on?"

"These gentlemen are here to pick up our little Carl."

As we heard Carlisle's nickname, Kol and I exchanged a grin, while Carlisle shook his head and rolled his eyes.

"Is that so?"

"Mom, this is Kol and Tristan."

"I know who the heirs are." She brushed him off. "The question is, where are they taking you?"

He didn't answer. Instead, he glanced at us with an uncertain expression. Adelle let out a frustrated sigh. "They're here. Take him to his mate. I've been telling him to go to her, but he's been a stubborn ass." She reached over and smacked the side of his head.

"Ouch! Quit doing that," Carlisle complained.

"Well, you deserve it. You are very stubborn," his mom said.

"But you guys need me. It's not safe. You know Lucille will be targeting our coven."

Adelle's eyes flashed. Gone were the gentle ones. She looked more like her sister now. "I told you not to mention that evil wench's name in this house."

Carlisle's mom took his hand, and in a gentle tone, she said, "We can take care of ourselves. Plus, if they manage to take us, we want you far away from their clutches. You know they've been targeting you since you were a baby. You're a threat to her."

Carlisle dislodged her hold and shook his head.

"Let me finish," his mom said sternly. "If you are one of Viola's mates, then you need to be with her. I also think by her side is the safest place for you."

"Linda is right. There is a reason she chose you all as her mates. She needs every one of you to stabilize her powers.

Without her mates, we have no chance of her defeating the traitors."

"What do you mean?" Kol asked.

"Is there anything you can tell us to help Vi?" I followed.

"Carlisle can tell you everything you need to know," Adelle said as she stared at Carlisle, daring him to argue once again.

His shoulders sagged in defeat, but in a last-ditch effort, he said, "But what about the children? Who will protect them?"

"Carl, stop worrying. Suppose the worse comes to pass. I am confident you will save us," his mother said.

"Yeah, plus they won't hurt us. We are what you call leverage," Adelle said with fire in her eyes.

I liked her. She wasn't at all like her traitorous sister.

Carlisle didn't look convinced.

"We don't have much time. We need to be out of Casters' territory before first light." Kol tried to keep the irritation out of his voice, but there was still an edge to his tone.

"It's settled then," Adelle said before jumping off the stool. "Kids!"

The kitchen filled with several teenagers, school-age kids that ranged from about age five to ten, and two other men—one of them resembled Carlisle. He stepped next to Linda and placed a hand on her shoulder. "What's going on?"

"A Vampire."

"A Shifter."

The kids whispered to each other as they eyed us with curiosity. The kids took a step closer to us, but the teens held them back.

"It's okay. They're friends," Carlisle said dismissively as he continued to have low conversations with the adults.

I lost track of what was being said since little hands swarmed Kol and me, curiously touching and prodding us to check if we were real.

Someone tugged on Kol's shirt, and I looked down at a little boy with messy dark hair. "Do you have fangs?" he asked.

"Ty, you don't ask a Vampire if he has fangs. It's rude," a teenage girl with blue eyes and red hair said, but she eyed me from under her lashes.

Kol squatted down so I would be at eye level with the boy. He reached up and pulled Kol's lip up to peek if I had fangs. Kol laughed and said, "They not there unless I need them."

A boy, probably around eight years old, stood next to me. "Like Shifters' claws. They retract as well." He glanced at my hands as if waiting for it to show.

"I want to see."

"Yes. I want to see."

"Can we see?"

The kids begged us while the teenagers looked at us expectantly. They no longer held back, their wariness long gone, but replaced with curiosity.

Kol and I glanced at each other, then he shrugged in response. My claws extended, making the kids squeal in delight while the teenagers pressed in for a closer look.

"Wow, they're sharp."

"Don't touch, Dee."

"I want claws."

"I want to see Vampire fangs," a little girl said, which made everyone turn to me. Kol smiled as his fangs descended, but before anyone came close, he snapped them back in place.

"Did you see that?"

"That's so cool."

"Kids, I didn't call you here to make a spectacle of the princes. I want you to go upstairs and pack for Carl," Adelle said.

"Why?"

"Where's he going?"

"I don't want him to leave."

The kids continued to argue while two little ones latched on to Carlisle's leg. He bent down and circled his arms around them, then glanced at everyone. "I promise I'll be back. Viola needs me right now, so I need to go to her."

"Oh, Viola. Your girlfriend," one of the teens teased.

"Where did you hear that?" Carlisle's eyes snapped to her.

"Son, everyone knows about Viola."

"Yep, the aunts and uncles gossip about you two a lot," the oldest teen said with a roll of his eyes.

"Oh, God. I'm glad she isn't here," Carlisle mumbled.

"Young man, I expect to meet your mate soon," Carlisle's dad said.

"She's no... I mean, it's not..." He turned to Tristan and me with a flustered expression. "Those two are her mates."

"Officially," I said, which made Kol chuckle.

"Kids. Go now. They have little time," Adelle said in a loud voice which had everyone moving.

"We will escort you off the territory," one of the men said.

I shook my head. "No need to risk yourselves. We have both Vampire and Shifter guards surrounding the area."

"Plus, we don't want to attract attention," Kol said.

"Okay, but this is the quickest route out of here." Carlisle's dad pulled a pen and paper out of the drawer and started drawing a map.

"Thank you. We appreciate it," I said.

"Is it safe to contact our men, or can it be traced?" Kol asked as he tapped on the communication device in his ear.

"Unless you have an amulet or a talisman, then you risk detection." Adelle rummaged through some drawers and pulled out some small bags that looked like fabrics sewn together, stuffed with something that was both hard and squishy. "Here, these will do for now. I will send better ones that will last you forever." She handed four bags to us. "Carlisle has one, and I will make one for each of his bond mates and Viola. In the meantime, you can use this temporarily. It will scramble the energy so no one can drop in on your conversations, whether it's through mundane devices or your bond. But beware, it won't last forever, and a strong Caster like Lucille could break through it."

We smiled in thanks, but Kol and I exchanged worried glances, which Linda must have noticed. "Don't worry. It will do for your mission for tonight and around campus. But as Adelle said, you will want to use the foolproof ones as soon as possible. We will make sure you get it before the end of the week."

I wanted to argue that they shouldn't risk themselves, but I wasn't sure if they would take offense to it, so I simply nodded and said, "Thank you."

"You're all family now. Your bond with Carlisle is stronger than blood, so consider us your family," Carlisle's father said.

"Thank you for your help and acceptance. We really appreciate it," Kol said.

"Yes. Thank you," I added as I glanced at Carlisle, who stared at the adults in the room as he tried to control his emotions. However, based on his red face and the little shine in his eyes, he was failing.

He stepped into his mom's embrace and murmured something we couldn't hear. He did the same to the others as he said his goodbye.

We thanked them again as they all threw out advice I had trouble following since they all spoke at once.

"Stay out of Thunderhook's property."

"Don't go east.

"Watch out for bats."

"Don't talk to animals."

I was glad to follow Carlisle out of the room since his family was overwhelming me. Carlisle's home was filled with love and laughter, while I grew up in the quiet walls of the tower with only Sebastian to keep me company. A pang of sadness and jealousy hit me, which Kol must have sensed.

I didn't have this either. But at least now we have Vi, he said, glancing towards the kitchen one more time.

Yeah. One day we will share this with Vi, I agreed, picturing several children with Vi, which surprised me since I never saw children in my future. Plus, we were still young, so children didn't fit the picture, but having Vi in my life had settled something inside me, and I would fight to the death to keep that. Even my bond with the Vampire heir had given me a sense of belonging that I never felt with anyone else aside from Sebastian. Even the so-called friends that liked to hang around me in school were fake. They only wanted the status that came from being an heir. My bond with Vi and the others was real, and we were one. It was solid and unbreakable.

Oh, yeah. I want twins. I felt Kol's amusement laced with longing through our bond.

I chuckled as I watched the kids who circled Carlisle with their arms wrapped around him. Two little ones came over to me and wrapped their little arms around my legs. I started and patted their heads. They then moved to do the same to Kol, who leaned down and returned their hugs.

The little rugrats were too innocent for hate. They needed to be protected at all costs from the greed of Lucille.

Agreed, Kol said, wearing a stern expression. I forgot we had kept our channels open for Vi and Sebastian, which meant I readily shared any strong thoughts and emotions through our bond, which I didn't mind. I trusted them with my life.

We each carried backpacks that held Carlisle's belongings, while he hauled a heavy duffel bag on top of a backpack.

"What in the world are in these bags? Your shoes and make-up?" I asked in irritation.

"It's all my stuff. I'm sure they left behind a lot of it since this was sudden."

"You know, you could have bought clothes when you got there."

"I know. My backpack has my clothes. These are some things we'll need." He gestured to his bag.

We walked out of the iron gates, and I felt the thick energy as we passed the perimeter. "How were we able to get through the first time?" Kol asked.

"The magic is smart, and it must have sensed your royal energy. It also scans your intention, and it strips any magic off you when you enter. If you meant us harm, the energy would have burned you."

"Well, our intel didn't include that tiny tidbit," Kol said, his tone heavy with sarcasm.

We saw movement to our right. In response, Carlisle quickly erected a shield around us.

"It's Amelia. They're good," Kol said.

We moved towards the shadows and met up with Amelia and her men.

"All good?" I asked.

"Yeah. No trouble. Everyone is on standby," one of her men said. I didn't know all of them closely since Amelia had spent the past couple of years away from the castle, but I checked in on them since I was a bit protective of my sister. However, the couple that I knew I trusted with my life.

Amelia stood next to Kol. "We've scouted the area, and we didn't see any complications." She refused to say names during a mission, so she came up with code names. "Are you all ready?"

"Yeah. We're ready to get back," Tristan said.

"Leave your bag. We will deliver it to your room." She gestured to Carlisle, who looked hesitant to part with his heavy bag. However, after a few moments, he set it down on the ground with a nod. He must have agreed that it wasn't ideal to be burdened with a bag while crossing the Casters' territory.

"Follow me, and I will lead you to the...."

"Wait, they said this is the fastest and safest way out." I unfolded a piece of paper and showed it to Amelia, who leaned down, along with two of her men, to study the map.

"Yeah, that's where we're going," Ren, one of Amelia's men, said.

"We will walk with you until the entrance of Briar Lane. From there, it should be a quick walk to the boundary line," Amelia said.

"Once you cross the line, contact us, and we will have your ride meet you," Tallon said. I knew him as one of the Vampire elite guards.

"Why are we splitting up?" I asked.

"All the men are staying put. We have a group strategically placed so that if shit hits the fan, we are well protected from all angles. We need to backtrack just in case we're being followed. Then we will evacuate one team at a time."

"Are you working with the Shifters?" Carlisle asked.

"Are you the last ones out?" Kol asked in concern since Amelia was like a sister to him.

She must have seen this because she shook her head, then turned to answer Carlisle. "Yes, we are working together on this. We need to be the last ones because we can be stealthy and fast," she said with a stubborn jut of her chin.

Kol didn't argue since there wasn't any time.

I must have missed a signal because Amelia's men scattered and disappeared into the night with no noise. She then gestured for us to follow. I glanced down and noticed Carlisle's bag was gone. One of the guys must have taken it.

We used speed and stayed in the shadows. Carlisle didn't have trouble catching up, so he must have used his magic since he didn't have our speed.

Soon, we were hugging Amelia goodbye. She and her men had impressive skills. We've been working with them since the war started and they were excellent in stealth and Amelia's fighting skills rivaled any elite guards. Watching her now was shocking. She and her men moved like ghosts.

I had tapped into my comms and informed them we had just crossed the barrier. It took only a couple of minutes to see the familiar van we rode to get there.

We were all quiet throughout the ride back to the academy. I worried about Amelia and the others, but there wasn't anything I could do except wait.

We got back to our quiet suite, which meant Viola was asleep.

Carlisle took the couch. He had said little and only grunted a goodnight before lying on it.

Sebastian knew we were back but didn't come out. He said Vi was asleep and he didn't want to wake her. He said she fought her sleep until the end, but he said he sacrificed himself to make sure she was occupied and exhausted.

We crawled into bed as the smug bastard flashed us a smile, and his mind filled with their time together. My hand tightened on Vi's hip as I considered waking her up so I could make love to her sweet body. However, Tristan hit me with a pillow and shook his head.

Yeah, I knew she was tired. I could wait until the morning.

Before my eyes closed, I heard a muted chirp from Kol's phone. I reached for my phone and read Amelia's message. *I dropped off the duffle. We encountered a minor hiccup, but nothing we couldn't handle. Everyone got out safely.*

I read the text over Kol's shoulder and nodded. We were both glad no one was hurt. *Thanks, Amie.* Kol sent back in response. We owed her and her men a lot. I was glad to have her on our side.

Chapter 12

Carlisle

VOICES NEARBY WOKE me from a fitful night of sleep. Not that the couch was uncomfortable, but my mind wouldn't shut down. I kept worrying about what I would say to Vi. I mean, did we just agree to the mating? I also couldn't stop worrying about my family since Lucille would certainly target my coven.

Rubbing the sleep from my eyes, I swung my legs off the couch to get up.

"I'm sorry, did we wake you?" Vi said from behind me.

I froze as the magic inside me drummed in my veins; it caught me off guard since I had been trying to ignore the call of our magic for months. Since the first day in combat class, I knew we were connected. It only grew the more time I spent with her, primarily when I trained her in magic.

Most magic bonds for Casters often resulted in partnership since the magic worked symbiotically and would enhance each other's gifts. However, what I felt for Viola went deeper than magic. There was a pull from inside me I couldn't explain.

I spent months researching what we had when I was secluded in our home, and it took me ages to find what I was looking for, but after hours of locking myself in my grandmother's library, I discovered Casters used to have true mates. This phenomenon didn't just happen to Vamps and Shifters. However, since the curse, Casters slowly lost their opportunity to mate until it had become obsolete. The last recorded mating occurred centuries ago. The possibility that she could be my mate floored me. Not wanting to get my hopes up too much, I poured all of my efforts into finding out what they did to her mother.

"Carlisle, are you okay?" She approached carefully, not breaking eye contact until her leg touched mine as she sat next to me.

This broke the spell I was in. I rubbed the back of my neck and cleared my throat. "Yeah, I was just..." I looked around at the others who stood around the breakfast table, watching Vi and me intently. "Did Amelia deliver my bag?"

Kol frowned while Tristan shook his head and muttered, "Idiot."

"Yeah, it's in the coat closet." Sebastian pointed to a door by the entrance.

I got up and hauled the bag on top of the couch, rummaging through it until I found the notebook I was looking for. "This was something that took me forever to find. I almost got caught by Lucille's men trying to procure this."

"What is it?" Vi frowned as she stared at the notebook in my hand while the three stepped closer and made themselves comfortable around us.

"This, amongst others, kept me preoccupied since I left the academy." I set it on the coffee table and pushed it closer to Vi.

She stared at it in horror, as if she knew the contents of the pages.

"What is it?" Kol asked, moving to sit next to Vi and placing his arm around her protectively while Sebastian and Tristan laid a hand on her in support.

For a moment, I stared at the three who latched on to Viola, and a pang of jealousy hit me. I shook it off and gestured to the notebook. "I'm sorry. I had to read it. However, I will leave it up to you if you want to." She met my eyes and shook her head.

"I knew from the routine updates we get that King Henry had told you about your mom." Vi visibly stiffened, and she moved closer to her mates. "I'm not sure what you were told about what they did to her under the Casters' hands, but this notebook contained detailed logs about their experiments."

Her mouth dropped, and her eyes shone with unshed tears. "I... I wasn't told the details of what she had endured. I'm not sure I want to read it."

"I understand. From what I gathered in the journal of one scientist, they tried everything from science to magical remedies in their quest to breed hybrid babies. They had some success, but they never fully achieved a viable hybrid pregnancy. Their experiments focused on altering your mother's DNA to hold all three species, which would have allowed her to breed with others successfully. Now, the last part is only a theory, but I think I'm pretty accurate in my assumption that although they altered your mother's DNA, they didn't count on the intangible."

They all gazed at me intently. "You see, plenty of humans and supernaturals don't achieve pregnancy. Even though they are medically able, it's sometimes up to chance, or some would say it's up to a higher power. I believe it's a bit of both, but the most important factor is that both parties are bonded to achieve pregnancy. It doesn't have to be a mate bond." I gestured to them. "But some kind of strong bond, whether it's an intense physical bond, mental, emotional, or spiritual. That's the component the Casters missed."

Silence met me, so I continued. "The Casters pumped a lot of magic into your mother, and coupled with your parents' bonding, resulted in birthing you. They achieved what the Casters had spent years researching." I smiled at Vi gently, waiting for some reaction. When I still got none, I continued to talk to fill the uncomfortable silence. Was I wrong about sharing this with her?

"I also researched Mimics and Siphons, but from what I gathered, they were hybrids who were born naturally from interspecies mating."

I saw the frown cross Sebastian's face, and Kol shook his head in disbelief. "I know it sounds impossible, so I did more digging. I found consistent evidence that, back in the day, interspecies breeding was normal. Several theories referred to the curse as the reason it's no longer possible. When the witches hunted down the other magical species to extinction, the ability to mate with others also perished. Casters also lost the chance to find their true mates. It reduced us to only having magical partners, which rarely led to any deep emotional bond." I bowed my head in sorrow and worried that my bond with Vi was the same.

I never knew how much I wanted our bond to be a true mate's bond until I laid eyes on her once again and realized how I wanted to be part of their group. It used to bother me, seeing the Shifters parade their mate, but now that Kol joined the group, something inside of me ached for the missing bond.

Vi got up and sat next to me; I looked up at her as she took my hand in hers. My energy surged to the surface of my skin, reaching out to touch Vi's magic. "Perhaps it's time for us to find out if the Casters could mate once again," she whispered, and gazed at me from under her lashes.

My chest thundered with her words, and I couldn't help but admire how adorable she looked with the pink tinge of her skin. My hand ached to reach over and grab her close, to capture her lips and claim her. So I cleared my throat instead and asked, "How do you suggest we do that?" I tried to clear the huskiness in my voice, but my words still came out heated.

Her pupils grew as she met my eyes, and her lips pulled into a smile.

"Okay then," Tristan said as he got up from behind the couch. I hesitantly glanced at the three, worried I would see jealousy, but they all met my eyes and held them as if they were trying to give me support and encouragement.

"We'll give you two some privacy." Kol touched Sebastian's leg.

"Yeah, okay. We'll be in class." He tapped his temple. "You know how to reach us if needed," he said to Vi.

We both nodded absently, but Vi's eyes hadn't left mine as she continued to hold my hand.

After a few heartbeats of silence, I rubbed my nape in discomfort. "So... hh... how do we do this exactly?"

Vi laughed, which caused my stomach to flutter.

Then she released my hand and looked away. My hand trembled, wanting to reach for hers. I balled both my hands into fists.

"I... well, with the others..." She gestured towards the door that her mates disappeared through. "Well, our bond happened during... well, during physical contact." Her face flushed red, and she leaned her head on the back of the couch with embarrassment.

Losing the battle with myself, I reached for her hand and rubbed the top of it with my thumb. "We don't have to rush this. It can happen naturally," I whispered.

She moved to face me, which had our knees touching. Suddenly, all I could think of was reaching over and kissing her.

"Don't you want to?" she murmured as my eyes were mesmerized by her wet, deep pink lips.

I heaved in a breath and leaned closer, leaving a few inches between our lips. It was as if I didn't have control over my body. It did what it wanted with no second thoughts. "What are you asking me, Vi?"

"I... nothing." She tried to pull her hand away, but I held on.

"If you're asking me if I want you, I think you know the answer to that. However, I don't want to rush you into something you aren't ready for. I want this to happen naturally. We shouldn't force it."

"I want to," she whispered, then looked up with vulnerability in her eyes. "Don't you want to?"

Instead of assuring her again, I leaned closer and captured her lips with mine. She responded by wrapping her arms around my neck, so I deepened the kiss and pulled her closer.

Damn, she tasted good. The energy inside me tingled on my skin and heated my body. It was like my magic took control of my brain and all rational thought left me. Hesitation gone. I wanted more of her, and the need to taste every inch of her increased. I felt her energy respond to mine, and the result was intoxicating.

I laid her on the couch and dragged my lips to her neck. The sting of her magic shot straight into my groin. The moan that left her mouth encouraged my greedy hands.

It was too much, and the sensation overwhelmed me. If we didn't slow down, this would be over before I got to enjoy her thoroughly, so I pulled both her hands above her head, but the arm of the couch was in the way, so I picked her up and walked us to the bedroom as I kept my lips on hers. I kicked the door closed and headed straight to the enormous bed.

I paused and watched her sprawled on the bed, face flushed, chest heaving in deep breaths, and her pebbled nipples poking through her shirt.

"Don't move unless I tell you to," I commanded as I stripped off my clothes and left the boxers on. She lifted her head to watch me, but I admonished her. "If you don't follow my command, we stop. Got it?"

Her eyes heated, and she nodded.

I reached for her hand and kissed the inside of her wrist, then placed it above her head. Then I did the same with the other. "Keep your hands up here and don't move them."

She nodded, but her hips pressed against mine. I smirked and wagged my finger at her as I got off her. She wore a sleep shirt and tiny shorts that exposed her legs. I traced a finger from her ankle to her inner thigh and did the same to the other.

Then I ripped her shirt off her, which displayed her rounded breasts. She opened her mouth, but I stopped her. "Nope, not a word. Unless I say so."

She obeyed by clamping her lips together, which made me want to have those lips wrap around my shaft. Instead, I focused on the gorgeous woman in front of me and reached to flick her hardened nipples.

Her back arched, and she moaned in pleasure. I continued to punish her breasts with my fingers, lips, and teeth. When her moans got louder and her hips continued to squirm under me, I knew she was more than ready. I reached between us, and I almost lost control as I felt her soaking through her panties. I moved the fabric aside and swirled my finger over her wetness.

"Argh," she said between moans as her hips met my finger. Her hands lifted, but she remembered to keep them above her head.

"Did you want more?"

She nodded.

"Tell me what you want."

"You. I want you."

"How do you want me?"

"I need to come. I want you inside of me," she panted as I moved my hand faster.

"Don't come until I tell you to," I said as I ripped the panties off her.

Her moans were getting louder, and she was losing control. When I felt her quiver under me, I stopped. "What did I say?"

"Please."

"Tell me. Did you want to come with my finger, mouth, or my dick?"

"I want you." She didn't really answer me, but she had been a good girl so far, so I acquiesced. I was inside of her in one thrust, and she let out a loud moan. Fuck, she felt good. I wanted to play longer and prolong our time since I had envisioned this moment for months, but I didn't think I could last.

I thrust deeper and faster, and soon, I felt her convulse, and the sting of her nails dragged deeply on my shoulder. She broke my rule, so when she recovered. I flipped her over on all fours, pounded her mercilessly, and smacked her ass twice, which had her flinching but pushing against me simultaneously. "This is your punishment for coming before I told you to." She moaned in response, and after a couple more smacks on her ass, she exploded again, which pleased me since it assured me she liked it rough.

I wouldn't last much longer, so I pulled her to sit on top of me so I could look into her eyes. "What's my name?"

"Carlisle," she said in a husky voice.

I loved hearing my name as she gazed at me with a sultry look.

"I'm close. I want you to come one more time," I said and reached between us. She dropped her head back as she continued to ride me. It was the sexiest thing I'd ever seen in my life. I felt her tighten. "Come for me, baby."

She obeyed and took over by grabbing her waist and thrusting faster. "That's it, baby, you feel so good. You're going to make me come."

"Oh. God. Yes," she said. Then she pulled me closer and bit into my shoulder. I flinched in surprise, but then pleasure coated my veins, and I grunted my release.

I dropped onto the bed with her on top of me. Fucking hell. I had no words to describe the intensity of our mating.

I brushed her hair off her face and asked, "Are you okay?"

She nodded. "That was fucking amazing." I leaned down and kissed the top of her head.

We didn't move until our heart rate was back to normal. I continued to trace her skin with my fingers, but then I felt something that made me stop. "I can feel you," I said in awe.

She sat up and gazed deep into my eyes. "Yes. I can feel our bond. Just like the others. Soon we'll be able to communicate telepathically." She grinned.

I captured her lips and kissed her deeply. "I never thought it was possible to have a true mate. Thank you!" I said in between kisses.

"I think I knew you were mine from the beginning. I felt a bond to all four of you but didn't know what it was."

"I felt the same way. I had been drawn to you, beyond the magic, since the day in combat class."

I moved us higher in bed to get more comfortable and we lay side by side. My hands hadn't left her skin. "I'm sorry. It took me a while to figure out what I wanted."

"You mean you didn't want our bond at first?" She lifted her head and met my eyes.

"No. It's not that. I didn't want to get my hopes up and have another thing taken from me."

I trailed kisses on her jaw, unable to stop touching and kissing her. I could feel the bond getting stronger. My energy was calm, finally satisfied to be joined with hers.

I refused to think about what Lucille Pruitt stole from my family—from me. The head coven should have been mine, but she stole it by cheating.

Vi must have sensed my dark thoughts, so she pressed her chest into mine, which had me hardening once again, and said, "So, you're pretty dominating, even in bed."

I laughed and pulled her underneath me, ready for round two.

Chapter 13

Vi

MY OTHER THREE MATES walked into the bedroom and found Carlisle and I holding each other, half asleep.

"Glad you two worked it out." Tristan smirked.

"I guess I have to get used to being naked around you three, huh?" Carlisle dropped his head on the pillow.

"You need to get used to more than that." Kol crawled on the bed and tugged on my hip, pulling me away from Carlisle. "I can smell the sex in this room, and I can't think until I've had you." He then captured my lips as his hand dipped between my legs. His lips continued to travel down to his favorite spot on my neck—on the area he liked to bite me.

I stiffened, which he must have felt because he looked at me in question.

I pulled away and glanced at Carlisle, uncertain how he felt about this. I mean, everything was moving so fast with him. I wanted to make sure we didn't scare him away.

"I admit this is weird since I don't necessarily like these pricks." He pointed to the others, observing Kol as he sat up and leaned on the headboard.

Kol didn't look concerned but continued to rub between my legs and trace his mouth on my neck.

"Don't worry about me. This is actually turning me on," Carlisle said as he grabbed between his legs, stroking his shaft.

I turned to the two princes, who were already stripping out of their clothes.

Kol took that as his cue and bit into my neck, which had me screaming out a release.

"Holy shit." Carlisle said.

"I'm not done with you yet," Kol murmured as he stripped off his clothes and passed me to Sebastian, who eased me onto his erect shaft. As I sank onto him with a groan, Kol moved behind me and slid inside me. Tristan pulled my head to his hard steel, and I obliged by wrapping my mouth around it as Sebastian and Kol moved in a rhythmic pace. I pulled away from Tristan as my walls tightened, but I replaced my mouth with my hand. I spared a glance at Carlisle, who frantically pumped his hand and looked at me with molten eyes. The four of my mates, in pleasure, had me screaming out an intense orgasm. Tristan pushed my hand away and grabbed the back of my head. I opened my mouth as he plunged into my mouth.

I closed my eyes and savored the feeling of my mates. I felt someone pull my hand and wrap it around manhood as I felt Carlisle's energy join ours. Something clicked inside me. My whole body sizzled as four bonds locked into place. Our energy roared and overpowered my being, which made me lose control for a heartbeat, but in the next breath, it slammed into me, and I was screaming out the most intense orgasm I had ever felt in my life.

"Holy fuck!"

"What was that?"

"Did I die?"

"Wow."

"Is it always like that?"

When I could feel my limbs again, I looked up and saw my mates lying in bed next to me.

"What happened?" Kol asked.

"I don't know. Did you guys feel that too?" I sat up and leaned on so Carlisle's chest.

"Yeah, I felt that," he said, draping his arm around my stomach.

"I think we completed our bond," Sebastian said.

"That was freaking intense." Tristan reached a shaky hand towards me.

We lay quietly next to each other, basking in each other's company and savoring our bond with each other.

I love you all, I said through our bond.

Carlisle shot up, dislodging my head on his chest. "I heard you. Holy shit, we're true mates." He grabbed my head and captured my lips. His kiss broke, and his head tilted to the side. "Is that?" He looked at the other three, who wore identical smirks. "We can communicate with each other as well?" Carlisle asked, shocked.

"Yes. The bond mates also can communicate telepathically." Kol moved to the head of the bed, tugging me between his legs.

I cocked a brow. "You doubted our mating?"

"No." He gestured to us. "But, hearing you in my head just solidified it." He grinned, reaching for my hand.

Tristan moved next to me, draping his arm on my stomach while Sebastian moved to the other side, all four of us pressed to each other.

Carlisle kneeled in front of us and said, "Another thing I stumbled across during my research was the reason Viola needs all four of us." He grabbed my foot and started rubbing it.

"What?" Kol's fingers wrapped around my hair.

"What did you find?" Sebastian traced a circle on my stomach.

Tristan placed a pillow over Kol's leg to lie closer to my shoulder, with his arm wrapped across my chest. "I'm listening."

"I found that, often, Siphon or Mimics had several mates. The stronger the power, the more mates she needs."

Tristan lifted his head and lay on his arm to see Carlisle better.

I felt Kol stiffen up under me. "Go on."

"From what I gathered, each of us has a specific role. Vamps are to maintain the level of your energy, based on Kol's performance just now." He turned to Kol. "I'm assuming, and it's why you always want to mate with Vi and drink her blood. Every time you do, you level out her powers." He gestured to Tris and Seb. "Shifters are to siphon the excess energy, which Vi has a lot of. It builds up every time she gets emotional; that's probably why there are two of you. While I'm here to teach her control."

I studied Carlisle closer. "You mean you can sense my energy? I mean, I knew you could back then, but you sound like you have a deeper read this time."

"Yes. I already had a good read on your powers, but now, I can read your essence. It's the core of your power. Some call it your aura."

"So, wait up." Sebastian sat up but kept his hand on my thigh. "Should we be able to read her as well, so we know when she has an excess of power?"

"I don't know. I can show you what to look for. However, I think you subconsciously know when she needs release. It's why you're always touching her, and there are times you can't keep your hands off her."

"You mean it happens during sex?" Tristan asked.

"Well, yeah. Energies and desires are closely linked, so it enhances your desire when needed, allowing you to balance her power. I think as you learn to read her energy, you can do it actively and not have to resort to sex."

"Hey, I wasn't complaining. I say we continue to have lots of sex." Tristan grinned at me.

"I'm sure that will continue since, like I said, desire is closely related to your innate duty as her mate. As long as you have the desire for, Vi, then it will enhance that."

"We're all naked and vulnerable, and you're still a serious freak," Kol murmured.

Carlisle's brow drew together as the Shifter princes chuckled.

"I call it responsible. Besides, look who's talking," Carlisle shot back.

I rolled my eyes. Those four might have got along when it came to me and our mate bond, but they would always gripe at each other. "I'm hungry," I said, to stop their argument from escalating. "But I'm too tired to move."

"We can call in an order," Sebastian said.

"Can you do that?"

Tristan grinned at me. "We're heirs."

"What do you want?" Kol asked and gestured for Sebastian to reach for the phone.

"I want a sandwich, chips, and soda."

"Add some pudding to that," Sebastian said.

"And make the sandwich a double-decker," Carlisle added.

"You know I can't eat that much food."

"Please try. We need you strong for round two." Tristan laid his head once again and snuggled next to me.

I laughed. "Aren't we already on round five or six? I dunno. I lost count."

"Oh, baby. We are not done yet. This is just resting," Carlisle said. He slowly gazed down my body from head to foot, which had my stomach clenching.

My legs tightened in anticipation of having all of my mates inside of me once again.

I was getting addicted to their touch and their attention. I should have felt insecure that I had the attention of four hot men—all heirs, but I had learned to embrace the weirdness the supernatural world had thrown my way. With our lives constantly threatened, I cherished the good times and stopped dwelling over things I couldn't control. Of course, it helped that our bond allowed me some access to each of my mates' thoughts and emotions, which helped me feel secure over my mates' feelings for me. Even Carlisle. I could feel the contentment inside him and the dedication he had towards me and the others.

They might have had a habit of snapping at each other, but deep inside, the bond had erased any ill thoughts or feelings they had against each other. They were dedicated to the bond and each other as strongly as they were to me.

The physical proof was in front of me, and they were satisfied to be around me and each other. Although they had no sexual feelings towards each other, there wasn't any awkwardness in their closeness. It felt natural for them to be close. I doubted they would be as comfortable if I weren't in the picture.

Carlisle's statement rang true since their touch settled something inside me. I sank deeper into Kol and let my body relax. My eyes felt heavy, and soon I was drifting off to sleep.

I'm so lucky to have all of you in my life.

Chapter 14

Sebastian

IT HAD BEEN QUIET FOR the past few weeks, which made us anxious. Not wanting to worry Vi, we had our conversations telepathically or when she wasn't around. We planned for everything to ensure Vi's safety.

Even the students are behaving. I don't like it, Tristan said as he stared straight ahead, pretending to listen to Professor Taylor. We decided not to take any chances, so we officially changed our schedule to match Vi's. Carlisle sometimes even joined in on some classes. So, everyone knew Vi was bonded to all of us.

Of course they're behaving. They feared Vi, and now that we added Carlisle, no one knows what to make of our bond, Kol added.

I felt amusement from Carlisle, who sat next to Vi. We perfected blocking Vi from our conversations, but we couldn't block each other. What one heard, so did the rest. Thank goodness they couldn't hear every thought.

Do you think Mr. Tyler will speak more about the curse? I asked.

Maybe we can ask him since it's come up more than I like, Tristan responded.

Just ask me. I did a lot of research on it, the smug fuck said as he stretched his arm and draped it on Vi.

Kol, who sat on the other side of Vi, said, *We should speak with him privately. I don't want our curiosity getting back to unwanted ears.*

I hated to admit it, but the fucker was right. I looked around the room and didn't trust anyone except for the five of us. It was odd, but I trusted my bond mates with my life. It was like, yesterday, they were my enemies, but our mating with Vi had connected us.

Why are we wasting our time sitting in class listening about humans and the war with sups? Tristan asked in frustration.

Because Vi wants to learn, Kol said.

Her energy has been erratic lately, so this is good for her, Carlisle added.

His statement had us turning to him.

Vi caught our movement, so I played it off by looking at her.

Play it cool, idiots. We don't want Vi suspecting anything, Carlisle snapped.

Tristan turned to me and said, *I'd forgotten how much I hated the bossy prick.*

I nodded in agreement. Kol was serious, but he wasn't bossy. *What did you mean earlier?* he said, grabbing Vi's hand.

Haven't you noticed she needs us more lately? Carlisle responded.

Well, yeah, but it's because our bond is new, Tristan said dismissively.

No, you're right. Tris and I are getting extra action even after the four of us do our thing each night, I said thoughtfully. *The students are afraid of her, which upsets her. Our magical practice hasn't been going well.*

Why didn't you say anything? Tristan snapped.

I don't know. I thought she just needed to get used to navigating all four of us, but I started watching her closely. Why do you think I've subjected myself to this torture? Do you think I enjoy listening to this prick ramble on for over an hour? Carlisle pressed his nose to Vi's temple to settle his temper.

I want to sit next to Vi in our next class, Tristan demanded.

We ignored him, but I had the same thought. We all wanted to be next to her and avoided letting our competitive side get in the way since we didn't want to add to Vi's stress.

When the class ended, we lingered. Vi gave us curious glances but didn't ask questions. Kol wrapped his arms around Vi and rested his chin on her head while Carlisle kept a hold of her hand.

"Can I help you?" Mr. Taylor asked as he eyed us with amusement. I knew he was on our side and supported our mating with Vi.

Tristan was always direct, so without a preamble, he asked, "Is there anything you can tell us about the curse that might help us?"

Mr. Taylor's eyes widened, and he stared at Vi for a moment. Then, with a sigh, he gestured for us to take a seat as he locked the room. "I must warn you this might take a while, so you might miss your next class. I'll send a message to Mr. Wilson that I won't make my other class," he said as he pulled out his phone.

Tristan tugged on Vi's hand and sat her on his lap.

Mr. Taylor leaned on his desk, deep in thought. "I wanted to find the right time to speak with Viola about this, but it makes sense for all of you to be present in our conversation. I just haven't quite formulated the right words to tell you what I suspected. I've been dropping hints in my classes, but I'm afraid it's not sufficient."

"Get to the point, Gary," Carlisle snapped.

I rolled my eyes. Carlisle really was a bossy prick.

"Yes. I believe that everything culminating for the past centuries started with the curse. It's nature's way of finding balance."

"I beg your pardon, Mr. Taylor, but it's hard for me to believe that all of this is because of two lovers." Kol snorted.

"Yes and no. It's not just about the unmated Vamp and Caster. This is also about the annihilation of the other magical race. It's unnatural and caused an imbalance, and I believe the mates were the catalyst for the Casters to take power. Their abuse of power had severe consequences on all races. To correct the imbalance, nature had to counter it with significant power." He stared at Vi intently.

I felt Vi stiffen, and unease crossed through our bond, so I rubbed her hand, and Carlisle stepped closer.

"I've searched everywhere, and I've never heard of anyone having both siphon and mimic powers. It's also unheard of for one to be mated to all living heirs." He started pacing. "I suspected Carlisle to be part of your group long before but found no additional information. Because it defeats the purpose of heirs since, you're supposed to make sure the race continues to prosper, but being tied to one person makes little sense." He nodded to Vi.

"What are you getting at?" Carlisle asked, his hands on Vi's shoulders. We still felt her unease, but having our support was helping.

"I've scoured all history books. The best theory I've got is that Vi's strength should rival the power the Casters accumulated throughout the years, and you, as her mates, are to correct the imbalance."

"How do we do that?" I asked.

"You will bring unity to all supernatural races after Vi takes back power from the Casters."

"Why do you make it sound like the Casters have all the power?" Tristan asked with his brow furrowed.

Carlisle answered, which had us all turning to him. "Haven't you been listening? Throughout history, the Casters are the ones who always cause an imbalance of power by killing off other supernaturals. They started the recent war that brought attention to humans. Even now, they only pretend to acknowledge the Vamp and Shifters' rule. As you know, they had been increasing their powers. Look at Vi's mom."

"He's right," Vi whispered. A heavy silence filled the room. Then Vi asked Mr. Taylor, "How do you suggest I beat the head priestess? She has the entire race to pull power from."

"Unfortunately, you will need to figure that out with your mates. All I have are theories," Mr. Taylor said in an apologetic tone.

"Thank you for your time, Mr. Taylor," Kol said, standing up.

Tristan wrapped his arms around Vi's waist. I laced her fingers with mine as we walked out the door, nodding my thanks to Mr. Taylor.

Vi smiled at Mr. Taylor, which he returned warmly.

Thank goodness we missed combat class since we dreaded stepping into that room each time. So we went straight to the cafeteria.

Shay and Lori saw us approach and stole Vi from our hold, then dragged her inside. Vi looked back with an apologetic smile but with amusement in her eyes. We felt her happiness through our bond, so we slowed down and allowed her to enjoy her friends' company.

I knew Vi didn't have many friends growing up, so she cherished Shay and Lori's friendship.

Tristan stopped abruptly, and I felt Kol go on alert. I looked around and saw several students close in on us. I was about to call out to Vi, but someone whispered closer to Carlisle, "You wouldn't want to include her now, do you?"

We all glanced at Vi, who glanced back at us since she noticed we weren't following. "Go on. We just need to go do something for a bit," Carlisle said.

She nodded and smiled at something Shay said.

We can take care of this. She just now got over the last time she stripped their powers, Tristan said.

"Let's get on with it then," Kol bit out and stepped outside.

At least ten or more Vamps and Casters flanked us as they herded us away from the cafeteria. I heard the door shut. Glancing back, I noticed a few others stayed flanking the entrance, maybe to deter anyone from leaving or to ensure Vi was still distracted.

After a few steps, I felt a wall of energy close in on us.

We're trapped, Carlisle said.

Casters and Vamps surround us. Red-eyed Vamps crouched and had their fangs ready while Casters crackled with energy.

"Let's do this, fuckers." Tristan shifted seamlessly, and his wolf bristled in power.

Did you grow? You look bigger. I turned and studied Tristan's wolf, which looked larger and intimidating.

Not the time, fucker, Tristan responded.

Right. I shifted and felt energy sizzle from my snout to my tail.

The Vamp and Casters in front of us shared a hesitant look.

Cover me. I'll try to break the barrier. There are four of them maintaining it, so it might take me a while, Carlisle said.

I looked around and counted eight.

I like our odds, Kol said as his fangs descended, looking larger and thicker than usual. He blurred, and in a blink, the Vamp's head to my right rolled. *Holy fuck. I've never seen you move so fast.*

I feel good, Kol said in response.

Fuck yeah, Tristan said and leaped over the Caster, slashing, then latching on to another Vampire's neck. As Tristan landed on two feet, I heard a crack, then the Vampire's head thumped on the ground.

Well, okay then. We're doing this.

I tackled two Casters, but they were ready. One released an energy ball.

Watch out, Carlisle warned, but it was too late. I knew it would hit me as I saw the blue ball coming towards my stomach as if in slow motion. I felt the energy hit me, but it only stung briefly, which I ignored. I went straight for the neck and tore out his throat while I pinned the other with my paw on his face. I felt him hit me with some kind of energy, but it was like I was impervious to it. I swatted him in annoyance, and he flew several feet in the air and bounced off the barrier, then landed with a broken neck. I looked around and saw that Tristan and Kol dispatched the rest while Carlisle dismantled the barrier.

I thought it would take you a while?

He shook his head. *Not here. Are you okay?*

I nodded and glanced at Tristan for an explanation, but he returned my look with worry.

"I'll get the dean. Someone check on Vi," Kol called over his shoulder.

"I'll go. Stay with him." Tris jerked his thumb at Carlisle, who had four Casters in a magical binding. The area was free of students, so I had time to assess the carnage in front of us.

Coldness settled in my stomach. We took down our enemies brutally in just a few minutes. It wasn't that we'd never killed before. As heirs, we were constantly challenged. Since some didn't know when to back down, they forced us to fight until the death—it was the life of an heir, something we had to learn at a young age.

This was different because of how easy it was. It didn't seem fair, even though they had set a trap for us and intended us harm. It was unnerving. Was that how Vi felt?

Mr. Wilson came rushing with several staff wearing a grave expression. "We will talk about this later. I'll need to meet with your fathers." That was all he said before he sent us inside the cafeteria, where we found Vi finishing up lunch, unaware of what transpired.

"WHY DIDN'T YOU TELL me?" Vi scowled. Her bag was slipping off her shoulder. She dropped it on the floor, crossed her arms, and turned to us with her eyes flaring.

"Well, I guess we won't go to class." Carlisle sat on the sofa, struggling to contain the smile on his face.

"Don't pretend to be upset," Tristan said.

"Who's pretending?" Carlisle shot back.

We felt Vi's irritation flare. "Can we get back on topic here?"

"We handled it. We didn't want to involve you." Kol pulled Vi's hip close and tried to kiss her, which she dodged and shook off Kol's embrace.

I guess she's pissed, Tristan said.

You think? I said.

Carlisle straightened in his seat as we watched Vi in apprehension. We hadn't seen her upset at us. Not really. We annoyed her with our bickering, but it hadn't upset her.

"So, you battled others a few feet away from me, and I'm only hearing this now?" Her hands clenched into fists. "I don't know who I'm angry at most, them or you." She gestured at all of us.

Tristan got up and stepped towards her, but she held up a hand to stop him. I felt hurt and worry from Tristan, which was shared by all of us.

"Viola. Look, we're sorry we kept this from you, but we didn't want you to get involved when we could handle it ourselves. The last time you took on the students, it didn't go too well," Carlisle said.

Vi stared at him with a mixture of guilt and anger.

Way to go, prick, Kol said.

Ass, Tristan said.

What? We can't coddle her in this. She needs to know, he said stubbornly.

Well, you can be left in the doghouse, I said.

Yeah.

Yep, the other two agreed.

Vi's eyes narrowed. "Are you doing the communicating thing?"

"No," Carlisle said quickly. "Look, I'm sorry. We were just trying to protect you. If we needed you, we would have called." Her eyes narrowed in response, and his lips turned up. "Okay, probably not. Can you blame us? Our first instinct is to protect you. However, you know you would have felt something. We couldn't hide something like that from you."

I guess he didn't want to be in the doghouse, Tristan teased.

Good try, fucker, I said.

He ignored us and continued to shoot a pleading gaze at Vi.

"Fine. But what else are you keeping from me?" She sat on the single sofa.

Good. Now I don't have to kick your ass, Kol said to Carlisle as he sat down.

"Well, another reason we didn't call for you is that it was over quickly," I said.

"What do you mean?"

"What he meant was, we kicked ass," Tristan said with a smug grin.

"What these two idiots are trying to convey is that we seem to have acquired new strength."

Her brows drew together. "What? How?"

Carlisle crossed his legs and rubbed his chin. "I think it's you."

"Huh?"

He smiled at Vi's baffled look.

"That's the only explanation. As your mates, we're here to ground your energy. Where else does the energy go when we absorb it?" He left the question hanging in the air.

"And you've had so much excess lately." Tristan raised his brows and smirked. I wanted to smack him upside the head since he could take nothing seriously. He was either joking or angry with no middle ground.

"So, I strengthen you? All of you?"

"Yes. I felt the power thrumming through me. Something I've never felt before. I didn't know my strength, but it was like my beast took over, and he didn't show mercy."

"Great. So I make you dangerous?" she asked as fear spiked through our bond.

"No, I don't think you make us dangerous. But more power is running through us. Our basic instincts are stronger. So when we're in a fight, it's harder to reel back," Kol said thoughtfully.

"So these idiots need to stop picking a fight they couldn't win," Tristan said.

"What can we do to stop them?" Vi asked.

"I have an idea," Carlisle said, standing up. "I need to speak with the dean first." Then he walked out the door with no explanation.

"I hate it when he does that," Vi murmured. After a few moments of silence, she added, "I guess there's nothing else to do but go to class."

Kol pulled her close and pressed his lips to hers. "I don't like it when you pull away."

"I don't like it when you keep things from me."

"Fair enough, but you're getting punished tonight."

"Can't wait," she murmured in his ear.

"My turn." Tristan pushed Kol to the side, pulled Vi's face closer, and plunged his tongue down her throat.

I rolled my eyes and waited for him to release her. I picked up her messenger bag and held it out to her when she came up for air. I draped it on her shoulder, pulled her hip close to mine, and kissed her neck. "Sorry," I whispered.

She wrapped both arms around my waist and said, "You're forgiven."

Chapter 15

Vi

THE HEIRS STOOD IN front with Mr. Wilson and the entire student body while I sat with Shay and Lori during the assembly.

"... although there is violence outside of these walls, I would like to think we can keep the campus a safe place. We should leave the political turmoil to the adults and outside of our campus. I'm not saying to abandon your beliefs. All I'm saying is to keep this place a safe space." Mr. Wilson paused and allowed the murmur to die down. "To do that, I also would like to give our leaders a chance to say something." He gestured to the heirs.

Kol stepped forward. "I shouldn't have to be up here since my father's word is law, but my people don't seem to get the message through their heads, so I will say this once again. Back off and don't partake, or the punishment will be harsh. Look for my father's next decree about this complete nonsense. I promise you it will not be pretty since you have worn out his patience." Kol said it in a low and menacing tone. His eyes flashed red, which caused my arm hair to stand.

Tristan and Sebastian moved forward next. "This fight has united our people, which we've been proud of, and we continue to ask for their unwavering support and patience," Sebastian said.

"For the rest of you. You have seen what happened to those who crossed us. That's all the warning you will get." Tristan followed.

Carlisle stepped forward at last. "Although I don't represent all Casters, I represent at least half of you. We do welcome someone to come up here and speak for the other half. We want to implore you to stop the attacks on us, each other, especially on our mate. We will not back down, but we wouldn't start either. We are all here to learn, so let's do that. We should all work together to break the curse and start healing, not fight amongst each other."

Lori and Shay murmured to each other, but I didn't pay them any attention as I watched my mates proudly. They tried the diplomatic way, and it was up to the others to back off.

The buzzing in the assembly didn't die down, even while Mr. Wilson spoke and gave out a few reminders. I wasn't even paying attention. I continued to watch my mates and stayed alert in case someone tried anything. When we were dismissed, Shay and Lori walked out with me. "Hey, we'll catch up with you later, okay?" Lori said.

"Yeah. We have so much to do if we want to pull this off," Shay said to Lori, waving at me, but she continued to speak with Lori. I considered asking them what they were up to, but the crowd swallowed them.

I pushed my way to the front, but Kol got to me first. He reached and grabbed my hand and guided me to where the Shifter princes and Carlisle stood speaking with Mr. Wilson.

"Hi, Viola. Let's hope that was enough to stop any violence. At least for a while," Mr. Wilson said in a tired voice.

"I hope so too," I said, leaning on Kol's chest.

"Well, you kids get to class."

"Thank you, Mr. Wilson." I waved goodbye.

We walked to class and noticed several students stared at us while others flashed us awkward smiles.

A shifter, along with three large guys, stopped in front of us. "Glad to see you guys show solidarity and leadership up there."

"Yeah, it's about time," the other said.

"Hopefully these pricks get the memo," the large dude in front said.

"Thanks, guys," Sebastian said as Tristan nodded. They exchanged handshakes, and then we continued walking down the hall.

Is anyone weirded out by all the attention we're getting? I asked through our bond.

Speak for yourself. They always stare at me, Tristan responded.

Give it a rest, Carlisle said, while Kol and Seb expressed amusement.

We got through the day with no incident. Except the staring hadn't died down.

I asked the guys to bring food up to the room for dinner since I'd had it with the staring. Kol turned dinner to naked play for the rest of the night.

After a couple of days of hiding, I was ready to hang out with my best friends. I had received a few vague texts, so I hardly saw them. They claimed to be busy organizing something. I had a feeling they were dodging me, so I was starting to get pissed by lunchtime.

I picked up the phone and dialed Shay's number, which went straight to voicemail. I dialed Lori's, but it was the same. "Look, you two. I don't know what you're up to, but I'm worried and getting pissed. Someone call me back, or I might do something drastic. You wouldn't want that, would you?"

I called Shay and left the same message, and for even more dramatic effect, I sent the same text message to our group text. Sure enough, they both responded in less than five minutes, apologizing and asking me to meet them after school at the old building behind the library.

I showed my mates the text. "What do you think those girls are up to?"

"Only one way to find out," Seb said.

"You're right." I sighed.

I wanted to skip my training with Carlisle and hunt down my mysterious besties.

Training with Carlisle had transformed into more than magical practice. We'd been alternating my Vamp and Shifter energies and going against my mates, and sometimes we'd combine all of them.

My mates wouldn't hear of it. They were eager to continue practicing their newfound strength against me. I had to admit, it was great practice for all of us since our powers prevented us from harming one another but allowed us to practice at full force. It was like something nullified as soon as it hit us since it recognized the power source as its own or some crazy theory, Carlisle said one day. He had a lot of them. I tuned half of it out.

"Okay, Vi. Erect a barrier, please," Sebastian said.

I rolled my eyes since they loved to tease me about the barrier I erected that kept them out before.

"We're going to work together on offense, and you defend," Carlisle instructed. He had become our unofficial leader. Not that we wanted him to, but he was bossy enough and was very opinionated on everything, even in the bedroom. He loved to boss us around and tell us what to do as he watched. Kol was easygoing, but when he spoke, everyone listened. Except in the bedroom. There he was ravenous and dominant. Sebastian, I could never tell. He was an enigma. He could be anyone I needed at any moment, but I could trust he would always be honest and straightforward. Tristan took everything to the extreme, which inspired me to push boundaries and step out of my comfort zone.

"Vi, are you listening?" Sebastian asked.

"Yes." I waved a hand.

"Vi," Carlisle interrupted.

"Oh, right." I dropped my hand and concentrated on creating a barrier without giving away what I was trying to do. He said this was one advantage of an advanced magic user. Don't give away your move; otherwise, your opponent will have the chance to counter. The barrier shimmered in place, and Carlisle moved to the center. He'd been more attuned to my energy signature since our bonding, so I know he felt the barrier. I think the others recognized my energy too.

"Remember, don't let us touch you," Carlisle said.

"What do I get if I win?" I asked with my arms crossed.

"What do you want?" Kol asked as the corner of his lips turned up.

Oh, this could be fun. "Let me think about it." I studied my mates, who looked at me with a mixture of desire, anticipation, and hesitation. "I got it. I want to be in charge tonight. No questions. Total control."

"For how long?" Carlisle asked.

I smiled. Of course he would be the one who would have a problem. Tristan grinned as he met my eyes, while Seb winked. Kol met my eyes with a heated gaze, and I knew he would love whatever I had in store for him. So, I faced Carlisle. "How about thirty minutes?"

"You're a horrible negotiator," Tristan said, and Kol and Seb chuckled.

"Fifteen," Carlisle countered. I ignored the others; I knew Carlisle hated not being in control. Thirty was too much for him, so I needed to sweeten the deal.

"Okay. How about whoever gets a hit gets released early? But, if I win, I'm in charge for thirty minutes."

"Oh, that'd be me," Tris said.

"Dream on, brother," Seb countered.

Kol didn't take part since I knew he didn't care regardless, but I watched Carlisle as I knew he was just as competitive as the others but didn't like to show it. "You're on," he said.

I grinned and blurred to the other end of the room since the brothers liked to play dirty. I smiled back at the spark in their eyes.

"Wait. What do we get if we win?" Kol asked.

"Oh yeah," Tristan said.

I shrugged. "What do you want?"

"How about whoever gets a hit gets you alone in the shower, and if we win, we get to dictate every move you make tonight?" Carlisle countered.

"Oh, I like that," Seb said.

"Yes. I second that."

Kol's cheeks turned up in a panty-melting smile.

"Deal," I said.

The brothers shifted, Kol's eyes turned red, and I felt Carlisle's energy surface. I needed to watch out for Carlisle since he had long-range, but Kol was fast. I extended my shield several feet around me just in case. Their advantage was they could communicate and coordinate their attack, so I couldn't afford to get distracted.

However, I'd gotten to trust my ability, and I knew I worked best on instincts. I failed when I over-thought things, so I stayed alert but didn't focus on one thing. I felt Carlisle release his energy and saw a blur from the opposite side. I countered Carlisle's power with a block and expanded it in the blur's direction. At the last minute, I felt the brothers next to me, so I made my shield burst outward which had the brothers flying towards the barrier. Damn, they came out of nowhere. Carlisle lobbed a fireball as I saw Kol blur close. These guys were determined. They weren't giving me a moment. I wanted to win, so I needed to end this fast. Otherwise, one of them would slip in. Without overthinking it, I pulled the oxygen from within the barrier, and they all dropped in seconds. I wrapped them in my energy and released the oxygen as I pulled them close to me. I looked down at them with a smug grin on my face.

"How... how did you do that?" Carlisle took deep breaths and got up.

"Damn, babe. That was harsh." Tris bent over and leaned on his knee.

"Cool trick," Kol said.

Seb just shook his head.

"I'm serious, Vi. That's not possible," Carlisle said.

"What do you mean?"

"I mean, Casters have elemental magic. We manipulate the surrounding energies. So we can manipulate the wind, but we can't suck out oxygen to the anatomic level. It should have taken us a few minutes before losing our breaths, not instantly like you just did. It was like we were in space and oxygen didn't exist."

"I don't know. I'm a siphon. I siphoned out the oxygen." I shrugged.

They studied me like I was crazy.

"We know little about your powers," Kol said.

"I think it's cool." Tristan kissed my cheek. "Looking forward to what you have in store for us tonight."

I smiled in response, but my smile faded as I met Carlisle's intense gaze. He studied me intently. "Is there anything wrong?"

"No. But, suppose we knew the extent of your power. We could end this war before it even begins," he said in almost a whisper.

Fear and pressure suddenly filled me, which they must have felt since they closed in on me. "I'm sorry, Vi. I didn't mean to say that out loud. Of course we're not expecting that from you. It's dangerous to attempt such a thing anyway. However, we need to study your power before we push you, so we're not caught with any surprises."

I nodded, and he kissed my forehead.

Kol took my hand and led me out of the room as Sebastian took my other hand.

"Vi, do you mind if I skip this? I should get started researching the extent of your power more," Carlisle said.

I paused and studied our bond and felt no fear or hesitation from him, just determination to protect me, which I appreciated. He was right, and we needed to know everything about mimic and siphon before facing the coven. "Not at all. Do you need help?"

"Not right now, but I'll ask if I do."

I smiled and walked out with my other mates. We got to the back of the library as Lori and Shay instructed, but we found the place crowded.

What is going on? Tristan asked.

Are we in the right place? Kol asked.

Yes, I think, I answered.

Can you spot them? Seb peered over the crowd.

There. Kol tugged on my hand and led us to the front.

"Oh, good. You guys are here," Shay said.

"Yes, but stay here. Try to blend in." Lori led us to the corner.

"What's going on?"

"You'll see." Shay winked, while Lori shot me a mysterious smile.

"It's time," she said and gestured for Shay to join her. Shay grinned at me, and they both walked to the center. The crowd gathered around them, which made me nervous, so I walked to them. However, Seb held me back. I glanced at him in confusion and then back at Shay and Lori.

They were both smiling. Then a Shifter lifted her on top of a chair, which made everyone laugh. "Yes, well. Thanks for coming. As you know, we organized this gathering to bring everyone together. Shifters, Vamps, and Casters." She opened her hand with her palms up. "To bring forth a new future. A future of peace."

My jaw dropped, and I felt the surprise from my mates.

"Yes. Like us, I know many of you just want to learn and live your life without having to take sides. So this is what we're here for. We shouldn't have to live in fear. We're here to learn. Our families shouldn't be threatened if we don't pick a side. We're only kids." She paused and looked around as the crowd murmured their support. "There's strength in numbers. If we all get together, we can help each other and protect each other. We can make others listen," Lori continued.

"Also, if we make a stand, a stand for ourselves and not for those who seek power, then maybe they wouldn't be too eager to resort to violence. Without the support of others, they could easily be defeated."

The murmur got louder. "Even though it sounds like we're saying support the shifters at this moment, it doesn't mean we support them blindly. All it means is for this fight. We support them because the Casters will wage war and kill innocent lives to gain power. The Shifters did nothing wrong. When this is over, we will make another stand. A stand for equality. It means no more segregation. We are all supernaturals. The greed of our ancestors has punished us enough. It's time to break the curse." Shay's voice rose on the last part.

"Who's with us?" Lori screamed.

"Break the curse," someone said from the crowd. Then another. Then another until the entire room was chanting it.

Kol tugged on my hand, and we slipped out of the room. *We need to leave before they notice us and ruin what they're trying to accomplish*, he said.

Holy shit. Who would have thought my best friends would lead a revolution, I said in awe.

This is good but also dangerous, Sebastian said.

What do you mean? I asked as we made our way back to our room.

Well, if they get enough support and the Casters learn about this, they'll be a target, Tristan said.

I stopped and clutched his arm.

Don't worry, Vi. I'll speak to our guys and make sure they stick close to the girls twenty-four seven. Tristan kissed my cheek before turning around.

Thanks, Tris. I love you.

Love you too. I expect payment when I get back.

I laughed and clutched the elbows of Kol and Seb as we took the elevators.

Everything had gotten more serious. Everyone was in danger. I needed to step up my game and protect everyone I loved. Not just them, but everyone who just wanted to live normal lives. They didn't deserve to be caught in this mess.

Kol distracted me from my spiraling thoughts as he trailed kisses on my neck, but as Sebastian opened the door to our suite, we stiffened as we found unexpected guests.

"Amelia, what are you doing here, and how did you get in?" Kol asked.

She ignored him. Instead, she stepped in front of me and hugged me.

"Hey, I missed you."

"I missed you too," she said. "How have you been? Has Kol been behaving?"

"Yeah, mostly." I grinned.

"I'm standing right here," he said in irritation, but we continued to ignore him.

"What are you doing here?" I asked.

"Vi, you haven't officially met my team. This is Dimitri, Tallon, Renwick, and Owen."

"They're my elite guards," Kol interrupted.

"Not anymore. Plus, not all of them were yours." Amelia shook her head as Kol just glared.

"Sorry, man. Vi, it's nice to meet you officially," Dimitri said.

"Nice to meet all of you. This is Sebastian and Tristan, my mates."

"We've met," Tallon said.

Amelia sat next to Renwick and Owen, who moved closer to her. I eyed them closely as Kol's eyes narrowed.

Do you think they're together? he asked.

I don't know, I said, looking away.

I'm going to kick their ass if they hurt my sister, Kol said.

I tried not to show my amusement, so I focused on what Dimitri was saying. "...yesterday."

"The King agrees we need to be here if the Casters are planning on making a move," Amelia continued.

"The dean assigned us a suite just down the hall so we wouldn't be far," Tallon said.

"You mean, the five of you are sharing a room?" Kol asked.

"It's not the first time," Amelia said. "It's what we do when we're on a mission."

Kol stared at each of the guys, who didn't meet his eyes. I tried nudging his knee with mine, but he didn't stop glaring.

"Keep us up to date with what's going on here, so we know how to proceed," Amelia said.

"Oh, God This is gonna take all night," Sebastian complained.

"Did you have plans tonight?" Amelia asked with a cocked brow.

"Not anymore."

She flashed him a knowing grin, which I shared with her.

The time we spent at Kol's castle brought us close. I liked her. She was a no-nonsense kind of person, and most of all, she loved and protected Kol fiercely. Not to mention she'd seen me naked and had walked in Kol and me having sex several times. After that, there wasn't any shame between us.

My plans to dominate my mates that night didn't happen, but I enjoyed getting to know Amelia's men. It was evident by the end of the night that something was going on between the five of them, which put Kol in a foul mood.

Chapter 16

Vi

AMELIA AND HER MEN stayed in the shadows. They demanded it was best if no one knew they were on campus since it was easier to gather intel. We trusted them since it was what they did best. They advised us to act normal and to attend our regular classes but to stay vigilant.

We were in the library for independent studies when a commotion disrupted the silence. Several people in uniform marched in my direction, followed by a very flustered Mr. Wilson. My mates got up from their seats and surrounded me.

An old man with grey hair stepped forward, along with a younger lady, and he said, "Miss Price, you are under arrest for the attack of several members of the Caster family. Come with us quietly, or we will use force on you."

My mates stepped forward menacingly, but I raised my hand as I looked around the fearful eyes of several students in the library. There were too many innocent people around. I don't want anyone to get hurt.

"As I said, you don't have any jurisdiction to arrest Miss Price." Mr. Wilson walked around the Caster and stood between us.

Contact the Kings now, Carlisle said through our bond. Kol and Sebastian moved so fast no one could stop them from leaving.

The Casters raised their hands in defense, waiting for an attack. Some moved as if to give chase, but the man in front raised his hand to stop them.

"I will not fight. Lead the way." I gestured to the door.

For a moment, no one moved. It was as if they were waiting for us to attack, then after a few heartbeats, they surrounded me.

Carlisle released his energy, and Tristan shifted as they fought to be by my side.

A dozen Casters held them back while Mr. Wilson and I begged for my mates to stop. After a few minutes of chaos and panic, my mates must have heard my plea because they gave up and agreed to walk behind everyone. I let out a breath of relief and released the magic I was ready to use to defend my mates.

I could feel my mates' frayed tempers, so I sent calming thoughts through our bond. *Guys, this is not the place to fight. There are too many innocent bystanders,* I begged.

Tristan continued in his wolf form, and Carlisle's energy stayed on the surface.

The Casters close to my mates were on edge. The one close to Carlisle dropped an energy ball when the door to the library slammed. I could feel Carlisle's sizzling energy from where I was.

As we walked, we drew a crowd.

Every shifter we passed kept their eyes averted as Tristan was broadcasting his Alpha energy to everyone. Some even kneeled since they could feel the hostility pouring out of him.

I could feel their anger through our bond, so I tried to keep mine in check. I didn't want to trigger them further. I looked back and saw every shifter follow us as a show of solidarity.

The Casters glanced behind us and must have noticed them as well since they exchanged nervous glances.

I didn't hear Tristan command them to follow, but they must have instinctively followed their Alpha. Tristan's Alpha energy sizzled with every step. His tail moved stiffly from side to side, his fangs bared and ears erect.

I was confident my guys could take down a dozen guards sent to detain me in the blink of an eye. So I kept my head low and followed the Casters' lead. I didn't want to start the war prematurely.

However, panic rose in me as I noticed the Casters were leading me off-campus.

I glanced at Mr. Wilson with worry, but before we could take action, Kol, Sebastian, Amelia, and her men blocked our way.

"You are not taking her off-campus," Kol said. I let out a relieved breath.

"She is under arrest—"

"We heard you the first time. However, as Mr. Wilson tried to tell you, she isn't a Caster, so you have no authority to detain her. We will follow the usual protocol for the crimes she's being charged with. We will detain her on campus. Security will take her." He gestured for Amelia to take her.

Amelia and her men stepped forward.

The Casters got into a fighting position, and energy sizzled in the air.

"I would suggest you don't do that. You are severely out of your league. Go back to your mistress and tell her to come do her dirty work herself if she doesn't want to follow protocol." Kol flashed his fangs. He gestured for Amelia, who bumped the shoulders of the Casters who were in her way as she and her men led me inside the castle.

My guys knew that if they didn't keep me in the loop, I wouldn't agree to go quietly, so they kept the bond wide open so we could share everything with each other. It was something we'd practiced many times—our way of communicating without words.

I saw from our bond that the Kings were informed, and they were on their way.

Heavy tension hung in the air. The bald man and the female looked around and realized we outnumbered them, so they agreed to the terms and addressed Mr. Wilson with the imprisonment terms and a promise they would keep in touch.

Tristan, who was still in his wolf form, growled, and the Shifters crowded the Casters. I was confident he gave the command to make sure they left campus. How did he do that?

He didn't relax or shift for a while.

Mr. Wilson glanced at me with an apologetic smile and led me to a room on the ground floor not too far from his office on the opposite wing. It had an iron door with minimal accommodations with a separate bathroom.

The room was large enough to fit me, my mates, Amelia, and her men, who stayed inside with us.

I crawled on top of the queen-sized bed while the others found a spot to sit on.

Tristan paced the room in his wolf form as everyone watched him in silence.

Eventually, the tension in the room slowly eased. Tristan must have received the signal from the Shifters that the Casters were gone because he finally relaxed and shifted back. "Sorry, Vi. We need to keep you here and follow the rules. Otherwise, the Casters will come up with something and twist it to their advantage." He sat next to me and draped an arm around my shoulder.

"It's fine." I shrugged.

"It's not fine," Kol bit out.

Sebastian sat next to me and didn't say a word.

Carlisle paced the room.

"Were you able to get a hold of the Kings?" Mr. Wilson asked.

"Yes. Father will be here shortly with King Rahl."

Amelia's head snapped up. "It's a trap. That's what the Casters want."

"We'll go and warn them," Owen said over his shoulder on his way out, followed by Renwick and Tallon.

"Be careful," Amelia said. Owen raised a hand in acknowledgment.

"What about Uncle?" Tristan asked.

"They will protect both Kings. They're both important," Amelia said.

Seb and Kol pulled out their phones. I assumed they were warning them.

If Rahl or Henry get hurt, I will hunt down every one of Lucille's coven.

Carlisle met my eyes and nodded. I forgot we kept our channels open, so they heard my thoughts.

"What now?" I asked.

"You need to stay put. Unfortunately, until we hear back from the Kings, we have no choice," Mr. Wilson said, walking towards the door. "I promise to keep you posted, Viola."

"Don't worry about me," I said.

"We'll patrol the campus and make sure the rest of the students are safe and we're not caught by surprise," Dimitri said, tugging on Amelia's hand.

"Kol, grab your comms, and Carlisle, make sure everyone has their amulets," Amelia said before stepping out.

Kol and Carlisle gathered our things while the Shifter brothers stayed locked up with me.

We didn't hear a word from the Kings for a couple of days. Amelia assured us that her men got to the Kings in time and they were safe. However, things had escalated since the Casters had failed in retrieving me.

"Ren is gathering intel on the coven. They got wind that Vi was getting more support from sups, so they bumped up plans before she gained more followers. We're told to stay put until we hear from the Kings."

"This is ridiculous." Carlisle rubbed his face. I could feel his worry and frustration, but also I could feel his fear for his family.

"We can't wait much longer, Amelia. We need to get Carlisle's family out."

Amelia studied us closely, then she and Dimitri bowed their heads close together and then stepped out of the room without a word.

My mates hadn't left my side. The dean took pity on us and had an additional mattress and chairs brought in. It wasn't as large as the one we had upstairs, but it allowed us to sleep next to each other.

Amelia and Dimitri walked in. "Okay, we know nowhere is safer than next to you five, but we also know the war is heading your way. As much as I want to protect you..." she reached for Kol's hands and glanced at me and the others. "...others need our protection. We'll try to get your family out," she said to Carlisle.

"Thank you, Amelia. Dimitri." Carlisle hugged Amelia and shook Dimitri's hand. "I really appreciate this."

"We'll gather intel while we're out and try to pass on a message, but before shit hits the fan, we'll try to get back to you guys."

I hugged Amelia. "Do nothing stupid. Call if you need us."

"Don't start the fun without us," she responded, then moved to hug Kol.

I smiled and hugged Dimitri. We had gotten closer to her men. Even Kol didn't scowl as often when he saw them intimately touch Amelia.

Kol extended his hand to Dimitri and shook his hand before they left.

I was sick to my stomach with worry. Not even the touch of my mates was enough to distract me.

"I heard that," Tristan said, but there was not enough energy to his teasing. Even he was worried.

We spent most of our time in silence.

"Oh my God. How are Shay and Lori?" With all of my drama, I had forgotten about them.

"Relax. We had the pack leader keep them on lockdown," Sebastian said.

"Yeah. They tried sneaking out to come to visit you, but since they started a revolution, they have a target on their backs, so they're on lockdown," Tristan added.

"Good. Please tell them to stay put. I can't get through this if they aren't safe." They had taken away my phone as part of my imprisonment. I was lucky to have my mates with me. They were only allowed because they were my mates, and they knew they would start a war if they separated us.

We spent most of our time in silence as we waited for the inevitable war. I tried not to worry about the safety of the Kings and Amelia and her men.

"When this is all over, I expect my thirty minutes to be doubled," I said to the silent room. "And I don't expect any complaints from you." I pointed to Carlisle.

My mates looked at me in shock, which morphed into a genuine smile that turned into laughter.

It felt nice to laugh. It helped ease the heavy feeling in my chest.

"If war is happening soon, don't we need to juice up?" Tristan asked.

"What?" Seb asked incredulously.

"I'm serious. Think about it."

"He's right. You guys are stronger after you siphon some excess energy from me. I surely have a lot from the past few days. We need to be ready."

"Here?" Kol asked.

"No choice. Vi can't leave." Carlisle said.

"Anyone could walk in anytime," Sebastian said.

"Bathroom." I pointed to the only private place we had access to.

We all eyed it with interest. "Good enough for me," Kol said and walked to the bathroom.

"Why do you get to go first?" Tristan asked.

"Called it first," he said over his shoulder.

"It was my idea."

"You can go second."

"Seb and Tristan can go second."

"What? Why are you taking his side?" Sebastian asked Carlisle.

"He needs to level her energy, then you two can siphon the excess, then I'll come in to control."

"Fine." Tristan sat heavily on the bed.

A grin cracked my face for the first time in a few days as I followed Kol into the bathroom.

It must have been the first night in that room that we had gotten a decent sleep. It was dawn when a commotion woke us up down the hall. We heard heavy footsteps rushing towards the room and a heavy fist banging on the door. Carlisle opened the door and came face to face with a red-faced Mr. Wilson. "Hurry. The Casters made their move," he called over his shoulder. He didn't stop. He'd already pivoted to rush in another direction.

We scrambled to follow him, a million questions racing through my mind.

When we finally caught up with him, he said, "The Casters will concentrate their attack on this school, so the Kings are on their way. Our students are being evacuated along with the city."

"What do we do?" Carlisle asked.

"The Kings would like to brief you in my office. They should be there by the time we get there."

We dashed to his office without another word, but the Kings were nowhere in sight. It took another fifteen minutes of intense silence before they walked in the door. I rushed into Rahl's arms as soon as I saw him in one piece. Kol did the same and embraced his father. I hugged Henry as well, happy they made it to us safely.

"I was so worried," I said.

"You're the one they're after," Henry said.

"What's the plan?" Sebastian asked.

"Any news on my family?" Carlisle asked.

"Yes," Amelia said from the door. I gave her a tight hug. She nodded to Kol and then turned to Carlisle as I walked to sit between Rahl and Henry.

"I'm sorry, Carlisle. We tried to save them all, but the adults insisted on staying and fighting." There was something about Amelia's tone and the tightness in her mouth that didn't seem right.

My hand grabbed each of the Kings' arms, needing their support. "Please tell me nothing happened to them," I whispered in horror.

Amelia shook her head as I blinked back the tears that welled in my eyes.

"What happened?" Carlisle asked as fear-filled him, which I felt through our bond.

"Soon after we evacuated the children, they came and took every single one of them."

Carlisle bowed his head. I got up and wrapped my arms around his waist. "Are the children safe?"

"Yes. Dimitri is with them."

"How...?" Carlisle cleared his throat and swallowed a lump. "How about...?"

"Your family is still alive. They're being used as bait. Lucille knows that you're one of Viola's mates, and she knows you will rescue your family, so they intend on capturing you to lure Vi out."

Carlisle's hold on me tightened, his nails digging into my skin. I felt the turmoil and conflict he felt inside, which fueled the hatred I already felt for the evil bitch.

I *will annihilate every single one of them if they touch your family*, I swore.

My other mates closed in on me and laid a hand on me, which helped me control the swirling anger inside me.

"Okay. Everybody calm down. We need a plan if we want to beat Lucille," Henry said.

"He's right. That bitch is cunning, so we need to outsmart her," Rahl agreed.

"What do we do?" Tristan asked.

"The Casters have wired the town with the same explosive power they wired the castle with," Amelia said.

"What?"

"Are you certain?"

"We're screwed."

"How fast until you fully evacuate the people?" Sebastian asked the Kings

"It's important, but that's just one problem." Rahl and Henry shared a look.

"What other problem do we have aside from the death of thousands of innocent people?" Tristan asked.

"If the Casters detonate that much power, the humans will notice, and they will come in and nuke this whole town. Whoever escapes will be hunted until they put all supernaturals down like rabid animals. It will be the end of all of us," Henry said.

"Why aren't the Casters afraid of this?" I asked.

"Greed blinds Lucille," Rahl said with a shake of his head.

"So, how do we stop her and prevent the humans from finding out about this war?" Kol asked.

"Vi needs to negate the trap around town while we face Lucille and her coven," Henry said.

Before my mates could argue, Rahl added, "It's the only way. She's the only one who could do it, and we need all of you if we are to defeat the entire coven."

"She can't go alone. It's suicide," Kol argued.

"My men and I can go with her. I promise to protect her with my life. I'm sure my men would make the same vow," Amelia promised, holding Kol's gaze.

Kol studied her and nodded. "There is no other I would entrust her life to."

"That's settled then." Henry placed his hand on Kol's shoulder and turned to Amelia. "You and Viola negate the trap around the city. We will face Lucille and stall her as long as possible. Eventually, if she doesn't see you, she'll suspect something, so we'll need to make sure she doesn't leave."

"I got Lucille," Carlisle said.

Rahl and Henry shared a look.

I frowned and looked at my other mates, who also shared my worry. However, Carlisle didn't allow anyone to form an argument. "I'll have my bond mates by my side. We are strong. It has to be me that defeats her so that the succession will pass back to my family."

"You're right," Rahl said.

"Be careful. All of you. They have centuries of darkness on their side," Henry said.

"Where will you be?" Kol asked.

"We will deal with her people and make sure they don't slaughter any innocents," Rahl said.

"Our men are ready. We will make sure we rescue your family, Carlisle." Henry turned to Mr. Wilson. "Whoever is able, have their efforts focused on evacuation. Then, once everyone is safe, have them stay for protection. We'll send word once it's safe. If you don't hear from us, our people have contingency plans."

"Good luck." Mr. Wilson nodded to everyone and left the room.

"Viola, we should go. We need to meet up with my men before we can start," Amelia said.

I turned to the Kings, then to my mates for what could be the last time. Fear flooded me. "What about you? When do you meet her? Do you just wait here until she comes?" I refused to fall apart. I needed to be strong for everyone in the room. Even if I had to be in two places at once, I would make sure everyone I loved would make it out of this alive.

"We're meeting up with our people and coordinating our attacks," Henry said.

"We're splitting up the city, so we have the entire area covered," Rahl said.

I wrapped an arm each around Henry and Rahl's waists and buried my face on their shoulders. "Please be safe. One day, you will have grandchildren, and they will need grandfathers," I whispered.

They both wrapped an arm around my back and tightened their hold at the mention of grandchildren.

"You brought joy into our family, Viola. Thank you." Rahl kissed my temple.

"You made us a family again. I'm looking forward to being a grandfather." Henry kissed the top of my head. "You take care of yourself, you hear?"

I nodded and released them.

I ambled to my mates. There were no words, so I allowed myself to feel everything. The joy I'd felt with them. How they saved me from the darkness I felt after losing my mother and losing myself from the power inside me. How much they meant to me. They made me feel worthy and alive and, most of all, wanted. I found my place with them, and I'd have been lost without them. I needed every single one of them in my life. If I lost any of them, I would succumb to that darkness that once wrapped over me. I would give up everything if it meant I had them. Nothing else mattered.

We pressed into each other as we opened ourselves up to how much we all meant to each other. My heart filled to the brim to see how much they'd grown to care for each other. They didn't just get along because of me. They had built a genuine brotherhood.

Together forever were the only words I said before I stepped away from their embrace.

Together forever, they echoed.

The Kings wore bright smiles and shiny eyes as they watched us, while Amelia was flat out bawling. "I will gut Lucille if she breaks up this beautiful bond you have," she cried.

Henry pulled Kol into an embrace. "Your mother would be so happy that you found your place. I'm so happy for you, son."

"Thanks, Father."

Rahl pulled Tristan and Sebastian into a hug and said, "You have a lot to fight for. Keep your claws sharp, and don't let your fangs waver."

"You too, Uncle," Tristan said while Sebastian thumped his back.

The Kings stepped out of the room together as I lingered by the door.

"It's okay, Vi. We'll keep our communication open," Kol said.

"We'll wait here until the bitch arrives," Tristan said.

"We'll be ready," Sebastian added.

"Carlisle, are you okay?"

"They won't harm my family since they need them for leverage. I will kill that bitch before that happens," Carlisle said with determination.

Satisfied, I stepped away from the door and followed Amelia.

Chapter 17

Kol

"SHUT UP!" I SNAPPED at Tristan, who wouldn't stop muttering. "I might love you like a brother, but I will still kick your ass. I'm trying to listen so the bitch won't catch us by surprise."

"What do you think I'm doing? I'm communicating with Seb, who is linked with the other Shifters who are giving us updates."

"Will you two please stop bickering? I'm trying to keep tabs on Vi. Also, please tell me that Shay and Lori were smart enough to evacuate? We don't need Vi losing her shit." Carlisle said.

"I will personally drag them out if they didn't," Tristan promised.

Yes, I just got confirmation that their leaders are keeping a close eye on them and will make sure they stay put, Seb said.

From our bond, we knew Vi and Amelia met up with her men and were on their way to neutralize the Casters' trap.

"They're here," I said, shortly followed by Tristan, who said the same thing.

"Let's do this," Carlisle said, pushing off the wall forcefully.

The Shifters and I shared a look.

Seb stepped in front of Carlisle and asked, "Hey, are you okay?"

"I'm good."

"You sure? Because you can't let emotions get in the way."

"Yeah." Carlisle crossed his arms and squared his shoulders.

"You do stupid shit when emotions are involved, and when you get sloppy, it affects Vi and us," Tristan added.

Carlisle furrowed his brow and bit out, "I said I'm okay."

"You don't sound okay," I said.

"Look, I might be emotional, but I know what I have to do. I will never jeopardize Viola. Trust me." We felt the confidence and sincerity through the bond.

"Okay, man," Sebastian said.

"We got your back." Tristan thumped his arm and grinned.

I nodded and then walked out the door, followed by my bond mates.

It wasn't hard to locate where Lucille and her coven were. They came juiced up, and the air sizzled with their combined energy. The hairs on my body stood to attention as we reached the quad.

We stopped a few feet, facing the entire coven, with Rose and Lucille in front. They wore bright-colored leather garments that looked like battle gear.

Carlisle took point, but I stood close to him while Seb and Tris shifted to wolf form, one on each side of us.

"Well, well. What do we have here?" Lucille taunted with a malicious grin, which she shared with Rose.

"If it isn't my ambitious nephew," Rose said. "Trying to rub shoulders with the hybrid, are you? Do you think if you're part of their crew, it will make you an heir?" She chuckled, which was echoed by the rest of the coven.

I kept a close watch on Carlisle's emotions, but aside from a slight irritation from the uttered words, he still had the same determination to kill Lucille as before.

Good, keep your eye on the prize, I said.

"Tell me. Where is my hybrid?" Lucille asked.

"She said you're beneath her, and she has no time for you. So she sent us." I opened my arms and spread them wide as I smirked at the bitch.

Good one. Tristan chuckled.

Why are you taunting the beast? Sebastian groaned.

No, this is good. She's pissed, Carlisle said as he grinned.

"You four are cocky to think you can take on my coven." Lucille held her hands behind her back with an air of confidence as she paced slowly in front of the coven line. "You forget, we carry the full power of the Caster race, and you don't even have your hybrid." She paused and cocked her head to the side. "Tell me. What do you wish to accomplish with this suicide mission?"

"You think so highly of yourself, Lucille. You always have, and you always will. That right there is your downfall." Carlisle threw her a hard stare. "You see, the Caster race is divided. They've always been since you stole the power that was never yours. Our people were just too scared to correct the wrong you've brought not only to our people but to our magic. You upset the balance." He stepped forward, which I copied, making sure to protect his back. "Now Viola is here, they will rally behind her. Each coven that supports us is blocking your access to their magic as we speak." He paused and watched as

Lucille and her coven digested the information that was news even to us.

Lucille's eyes flashed while Rose's face turned red. The rest of the coven shifted in unease and no longer wore an air of confidence.

"By my estimation, you're about half-fueled. So, I will take those odds and see how you fare." He took another step forward as his energy crackled to the surface.

There was a heavy silence, and no one moved. Then Lucille cackled with laughter. "I've been at this far longer than you, little boy. Did you really think I didn't come prepared for all possibilities?" She waved her hand forward, and the front line stepped sideways, showing five people gagged and tied—Carlisle's family.

Don't show any weakness, Sebastian called as Carlisle moved to take a step. His emotions swirled in panic and deep anger.

No! Viola said through our bond. She must have felt Carlisle's powerful emotions.

Hearing Vi must have helped focus Carlisle since he breathed to get his emotions under control. His family kneeled on the ground with defiant expressions. Adelle held Carlisle's gaze in a hard stare as if to tell him to man up and get the job done. It was the same expression Amanda used to give Amelia and me when she was disappointed and wanted us to do better. The rest only had pride in their eyes.

"Give us the hybrid, or I kill them one at a time." Lucille gestured to her prisoners.

"Let's start with my goody-two-shoes sister. She was always a kiss ass." Rose yanked Adelle off the ground and held a knife to her throat, blood pooling at the tip of the blade from her struggles.

"We told you, she isn't coming," I said.

I'm fucking coming. Buy me time!

Lucille spoke once again and gestured behind her, but I stopped paying attention. I focused on Viola because I knew she would do something reckless trying to get back here.

Our bond didn't allow me to see through her eyes, but it allowed me to read her thoughts, so it was just as good.

Amelia and Dimitri were with Vi, as I heard fighting close to her. I felt an invasion in her wards, which made her flinch.

"What's wrong?" Amelia asked.

"It's fine. Nothing. The Casters are attacking the barrier I cast over you guys."

Amelia looked confused. "You mean them? Viola, stop that. Don't waste any energy. We can take care of ourselves."

"No one is dying on my watch." She shook her head stubbornly. "Now, let me concentrate. My guys need me."

Viola felt for the magical bombs that were protected by a handful of Casters. They'd only dismantled half a dozen, so they had a long way to go, so she felt for the same energy close by and latched on to it. Then she inched farther and did the same until she had half the city locked in. She pushed farther, but I felt the strain of what she was trying to accomplish. It felt like she was carrying a heavy weight that was pushing her down.

I wanted to cry out in warning, but I didn't want to distract Carlisle, who threw out some magical energy towards Rose, who had Adelle writhing in pain on the ground.

Sebastian and Tristan must have felt the same because I heard one of them let out a whine as the other pawed on the ground in frustration.

I locked in on Viola again, and I staggered backward as I felt the crushing weight she carried. *Viola had the energy trap of the entire city locked into hers. Her entire body shook in the struggle to hold the energy in place. She was on the ground with blood dripping down her nose. "Viola. Viola. Stop!" Amelia cried hysterically as she shook Viola. Amelia's voice sounded far away. Since I couldn't cry out in fear of distracting her or Carlisle, I sent out strength to both of them. It was the same thing Viola did before she left. I felt Tristan and Sebastian do the same.*

Viola took a deep breath, and I felt her draw into the energy we sent to her, and then, with a scream, she pushed up with her body and expelled the energy outwards that caused a massive explosion across the city.

I sucked in a breath as my veins sizzled from the force of what Viola did. My head snapped to Carlisle and the Casters.

Rose froze in doling out more torture on Adelle and shared a look with Lucille. The rest of the coven looked around, looking for the source of the explosion.

"No!" Lucille shouted, as she must have figured out what happened. She threw a massive wave of energy at us that had us falling on our backs but didn't do any damage.

Get her, Carlisle. We got your family, I said.

We got the other Casters. Kol, you're the fastest, so get to his family as we distract the others, Sebastian said.

Tristan didn't wait for further instructions. He leaped over our heads and tackled the front line of the coven. Sebastian followed as Carlisle, Rose, and Lucille engaged in a magical battle. I had to help clear the line since the fuckers attacked all at once.

Thank goodness, their magical attack didn't do any actual damage. However, the more hits we took, the more I felt the impact.

Eventually, one of their spells would land true.

I blurred, snapped necks, and tore out throats as fast as I could, while the Shifters did the same.

When I saw an opening, I took Carlisle's parents and blurred them to safety, then undid their bindings so they could free themselves.

Without another word, I blurred back in time to see Lucille and Rose join hands and blast Carlisle, which sent him writhing on the ground.

I tried to attack them, but I rebounded against their barrier, so I pulled Carlisle away from their attack instead.

"They're too strong together," Carlisle breathed as he wiped the blood dripping at the side of his mouth.

NO! Viola's blood-curling scream echoed through our bond, which filled my veins with a dreaded cold.

Carlisle and I got up, and as if in slow motion, I saw Adelle dead at the foot of Rose, who shared an evil grin with Lucille.

Sebastian and Tristan were only a foot away from them, bloodied, but wearing determined looks, ready to take down the evil bitches. Out of nowhere, Viola appeared behind Rose and reached for her head with both hands, snapping her neck. The resounding crack of her bones had everyone frozen, but Viola didn't slow down. She threw her hands out toward the Casters and screamed. "Carlisle, NOW!"

I glanced at Carlisle in confusion, but he stepped forward and threw spell after spell at Lucille, who deflected and returned her killing spells.

Takedown her shield, I called to Viola.

Sebastian and Tristan held on to Viola, who looked weak at the knees but wore a determined look as she nodded. *Be ready, Carlisle. I'm not sure how long I can hold it. Make it quick.*

I got this, he responded. I stayed by his side in support since I knew the Shifters had our mate.

Now!

Lucille made a wild gesture with her hands but stopped, and the energy ball flickered. She must have felt her shield collapse as she turned her eyes on Viola. With a screech, she threw several spells towards Vi, but it rebounded harmlessly. Of course, Viola would never have left us unprotected.

Carlisle ran towards Lucille. She threw several spells at him, but it didn't affect him. He landed on her with both his palms on her face and murmured under his breath. Lucille clawed at his hands, and within seconds, her body grew limp, and her skin turned ashy gray as she fell lifeless on the ground when Carlisle released his hold on her.

Viola's legs gave out, but Sebastian caught her. I blurred to her side and lifted her off her feet. "Release the barrier, love. It's over."

She smiled, and her eyes fluttered shut.

Carlisle kneeled next to Adelle's body with his head bowed. "Sorry for your loss," I murmured.

"Sorry, man."

"I tried..." Tristan started.

"It wasn't your fault." Carlisle cut him off. "Did the others...?"

"Yes. The rest of your family is safe. We tried getting to her, but Rose attacked us," Sebastian said.

"I need to get Viola inside. What did you want to do with them?" I gestured to the coven, who huddled behind us.

"I'll take care of them," Carlisle said.

"I'll stay and help," Sebastian offered.

"I appreciate it."

"I'll take the rest of your family to our room." Tristan laid a hand on Carlisle's shoulder.

"Thank you."

"I'll meet you there," I said as I blurred to the room with Viola in my arms.

"Kol." Amelia came rushing down the hall. "I wasn't sure where you guys were. Thank goodness you have her."

"What happened?"

"I don't know. One minute she took down the trap in the entire city and then passed out, and then she woke up and started screaming. Then she stood up in a panic and disappeared."

"I've never been so scared in my life. I thought I killed your mate," Amelia sobbed.

I laid Viola on our bed and pulled Amelia into a hug. "It's okay. I was in her head and saw everything. She saw Adelle die and somehow apparated here and killed Rose."

"She can do that?" She looked up with a frown.

"I guess she can." I chuckled.

"Oh, God. I'm gonna kill her when she wakes up."

"Fall in line. She was reckless today."

"But it's over?"

"Yes. The bitch is dead. How are Father and Rahl?"

"The Casters must have felt their high priestess die because they stopped fighting and surrendered abruptly."

"So, they're okay?" I needed to hear her say the words.

"Yes, they're fine. We had some casualties on both sides, but not as many as we were expecting."

I frowned, remembering the explosion.

"What's wrong?"

"Viola exploded the trap instead of neutralizing them. Now we have to deal with the humans." It's a worry for later. I'd take our win for today. I was just glad everyone I loved was safe.

"No. You don't understand. She placed a barrier on the whole city before detonating the trap. She couldn't just neutralize them since a handful of Casters guarded them. The humans and the sups outside of the perimeter did not know what was happening inside."

"Holy shit."

"Yeah. It was pretty incredible. Tallon and Ren about shit their pants, and Dimitri and Owen are terrified of her." She chuckled.

We were silent for a moment, trying to absorb everything. "She saved us," Amelia murmured as she wrapped an arm around my waist.

"Yeah, she's pretty amazing," I said as we both gaped at my mate.

I suspected she would be asleep for a very long time since she'd expended a lot of energy.

Chapter 18

Vi

"IT'S BEEN A FEW WEEKS. I'm fine!" I snapped. Frustration surfaced because my mates wouldn't stop fussing over me.

"Vi. We almost lost you," Sebastian admonished.

"That's an exaggeration." I crossed my arms.

"Well, you were unconscious for four days." Tristan tugged on my arm.

"Even the Kings were worried about you," Kol said.

"I just want to go back to school. I miss Shay and Lori. Plus, they said the people are getting anxious. They want change."

"Well, those two need to fix what they broke." Sebastian shrugged.

"Are you going to abandon Carlisle?" Kol asked.

I narrowed my eyes at Kol and stomped to the window. He fought dirty, and he knew it.

I watched the kids play in the garden. A smile lifted my lips, but my heart contracted in pain since I knew everyone in the house was still grieving for losing Adelle.

However, everyone rejoiced that the Caster race was finally free from the tyranny of Rose and Lucille. Not only that, when

I woke, Carlisle told me the good news–as the true chosen heir, the power of the Caster race now ran in him.

Rahl and Henry spent a few days in the mansion as I recovered to help guide Carlisle with his new role.

We buried Adelle a couple of days after I woke up, and we had been busy packing up the mansion to move to the Caster tower.

"Hey." Carlisle wrapped his arms around my waist and buried his nose in my neck.

I tilted my head to the side. "Hi."

"I heard your thoughts. Were you really planning on leaving me?"

We all promised to keep our thoughts open at all times. It was the only way we felt safe.

"I don't want to leave you. I miss my friends, and I want to finish school." I turned to face him. "I'm going stir crazy here."

He stared at me and sighed. I felt his mind churning and conflict rising within him, torn between his duty and the need to be close to me.

I cupped his face. "Hey. We'll figure it out. We don't need to be attached at the hip."

He chuckled. "I don't want to be away from you, Vi."

"Neither do I, but you're needed here, and you've done school. It's only temporary."

He let go of me, and I saw the pain in his eyes.

"Carl, don't be like that."

"You don't understand. It physically hurts me. The thought of being away from you for long periods is painful."

"It doesn't have to be long," Sebastian said.

"What do you mean?" Carlisle asked.

"Once you're in the tower, it's a short drive to campus."

"Yeah. We'll help you get moved faster so you wouldn't be away for long," Tristan offered.

"You'll do that?" Carlisle asked.

"Of course. Who else will direct us in bed?" Kol smirked.

I grinned at the shocked expression Carlisle wore, which quickly transformed into a smile.

"Deal," Carlisle said.

Which made everyone laugh.

I love you all, I said through our bond as we all stared at each other with love and bright smiles on our faces.

THE END

IF YOU ENJOYED READING Amelia and her men, order the Elite Guards on the next page.

Also by Lina Bengston

Subscribe to my newsletter to get updates on new releases.
https://www.subscribepage.com/linabengston

Amelia: The Elite Guards

I'M AN ÉLITE WARRIOR and a Super Spy. When it comes to relationships, I suck.

Growing up in the tunnels had its perks and downside. Instead of doing regular Vamp stuff as a kid, I watched my mom and dad work, which honed my skills.

Yeah, I was lonely till my parents adopted the Vampire heir. He initially intimidated me until I saw the Queen's cruelty. I swore then I would save my brother from her evil clutches and make her pay.

With my life mission accomplished and my brother happy with his mate, perhaps it was time to focus on my relationships. However, I'd rather fight in another war than try to untangle the web between my four elite guards.

Nonetheless, the new heirs are even more of a handful than their parents, so I'm sure I will be plenty busy.

The Elite warrior is the story about Amelia and her men. The timeline initially coincides with Magical Academy but will focus on Vi's children. This story can be read without reading Magical Academy.

Ananke: Primordial God

ALL I EVER WANTED WAS a simple farm life, but destiny had other plans for me.

When I graduated, I had it all figured out. I was going to spend the rest of my life with my high school sweetheart, and we would live on the farm next to our parents.

Until my unfaithful boyfriend betrayed me which unleashed something within me—it was mayhem that was so catastrophic that the fates had to intervene.

Now, I had to remain in a sanctuary to learn about control. However, chaos ensued. Because of my unstable abilities, I had to be anchored — to three powerful gods who were enemies and feared more in the sanctuary.

With their help, I've been able to curb the chaos. However, I must master my abilities quickly since my destiny is to conquer the evil slaying the godlings.

This is a fated mates novel with multiple love interests who are okay with sharing. Adult contents included.

Other Pen Names: P. C. Benson-Paranormal Romance/Urban Fantasy Author

COMPLETE SERIES

After many lifetimes of solitude, my mate is here at last.

Four years ago, I jolted awake by scorching energy flowing through me as the Savior's soul claimed mine. After several millennia, my wait is over—she's finally here.

Her arrival, however, foreshadowed a war between the Nephilim and the Fallen.

Since then, I've traveled the world in search of her, but she's been elusive. I know she's near—I feel her in my soul.

However, time is running out. I need to find her and keep her safe, regardless of the cost, since she's the key to saving us all.

Don't miss out!

Visit the website below and you can sign up to receive emails whenever Lina Bengston publishes a new book. There's no charge and no obligation.

https://books2read.com/r/B-A-MMVM-GMUMB

BOOKS 2 READ

Connecting independent readers to independent writers.